AND THEY JUST
KEPT COMING...

Two more office workers ran in, bent on throwing out the intruders. Raider stopped the first of them with a hard, chopping right hand. The second man tried to kick Raider...

"Your rules, mister," Raider said and dropped him with a much better aimed boot toe.

There was a mad pounding of footsteps on a distant staircase, and a moment later a swarm of more Florette employees poured into the office. There were six, ten... Raider quit trying to count them and concentrated on trying to keep them off of Ted Manton, who had fallen to the floor.

Rade kicked out blindly at whoever had him and was rewarded with a screech of pain. But there was another to take that man's place and another to replace the replacement, and more of them were still streaming through the boss's door...

Other books in the *Raider* Series by
J.D. HARDIN

RAIDER
SIXGUN CIRCUS
THE YUMA ROUNDUP
THE GUNS OF EL DORADO
THIRST FOR VENGEANCE
DEATH'S DEAL
VENGEANCE RIDE
CHEYENNE FRAUD
THE GULF PIRATES
TIMBER WAR
SILVER CITY AMBUSH
THE NORTHWEST RAILROAD WAR

RAIDER

THE MADMAN'S BLADE

J.D. HARDIN

BERKLEY BOOKS, NEW YORK

THE MADMAN'S BLADE

A Berkley Book/published by arrangement with
the author

PRINTING HISTORY
Berkley edition/July 1988

ISBN: 0-425-10936-4

A BERKLEY BOOK ® TM 757,375
Berkley Books are published by The Berkley Publishing Group,
200 Madison Avenue, New York, NY 10016.
The name "BERKLEY" and the stylized "B" with design
are trademarks belonging to Berkley Publishing Corporation.

PRINTED IN THE UNITED STATES OF AMERICA

10 9 8 7 6 5 4 3 2 1

CHAPTER ONE

It was wonderful. He remembered it all in marvelously vivid detail, and he smiled silently to himself as he did so, the rickety, creaking wagon swaying back and forth as the wheels crunched unevenly over the rocky road surface.

Oh yes, it had been wonderful.

The unnatural contrast of light and dark between the dark sheen of the silk stocking tops and the pallor of Beth's thighs. Even more, the pale, soft bulge of belly where the cotton bloomers had been torn apart. His smile strengthened as he remembered. He had not expected that round, doughy belly. But then of course it had all been so carefully hidden under the fluff of lace and crinoline. And, oh my, the dark, dark vee of thick, curly hair setting off the pure whiteness of her flesh.

But the way she *looked* had not been half of it. Not a tenth of the pleasure from this one.

Much more important was the feel of her. The sound of her.

The trembling as he touched her. The way her sobbing made her breasts heave and her belly quiver. The way she had tried to clamp her knees together when he hovered over her.

He almost laughed out loud but remembered in time and held his silence.

Oh, it had been lovely the way this one felt. The dry, puckered resistance as he pressed down and forward, pushing, pushing, finding the entrance and forging ahead.

And then that lesser but oh-so-important resistance after

1

he was already—if barely—inside the unwilling body. That lovely, indisputable proof that she had known no other. That she was his alone now, and for all time would remain his and only his.

That moment of resistance, then the tearing of her flesh and the release of her body to his. The penetration. Her sharp intake of breath at the pain and the knowledge. Oh, that was always such a grand moment. One of the very best although of course not *quite* the best.

Again he had to stop himself just short of the laughter that was bubbling up inside his chest. He struggled to maintain a straight face and deliberately gave himself over to the pleasures of the memory.

Beth. So young. Almost pretty. Certainly close enough. He smiled.

Her breath had been so hot against his face. It was lightly scented with salt from her tears, but she was brave. She did not cry out. He had warned her not to.

Again it was difficult for him to keep from laughing. The silly girl had believed him enough to keep from screaming even when he rammed through her virginity and impaled her on a spear of male flesh.

Stupid cunt.

Ah, there had been the pleasure of that initial penetration and then the wild, wonderful plunge within her, driving and churning and driving down and down against the unyielding floor of the choir loft.

He smiled softly, remembering that the floor needed sweeping. It had felt gritty under his unprotected knees.

Much longer and he would have wanted to stop and tear some of the expensive but no longer fancy cloth from her shivering body and pad his knees against the discomfort.

But it hadn't taken that long.

Beth had been so very good. She acted just right. The whimpering. The denials. The gasping for breath and hope.

He loved the way her own body had violated her there

near to the last. The way the dry, tight flesh of her softened and loosened and became moist.

Or was that the blood that was lubricating? He was never quite sure, and that was something of a pity, but then it was always best with a virgin. Always.

And that wonderful, wonderful finish. It could not have been more perfect.

The widening of her eyes. The ultimate stiffening of that soft but amazingly strong body. The rude, sudden clench of her flesh surrounding his as the tip of the little blade slid so slick and easy into that tender hollow under the curve of her jaw, almost immediately beneath the left ear.

Oh, yes. It was wonderful. Absolutely wonderful.

He was unable to suppress the chuckle that forced its way from his throat this time.

She had never even known the moment when her eyes glazed and her body convulsed madly and the bucking contractions of it ripped the seed from him in a paroxysm of the truest joy, and he was able to empty his body into hers in that final, perfect way.

Just thinking now about the perfection of it, the intensity of the release, the utter completeness of his satisfaction, was enough to give him an erection, and he hunched forward on the hard, uncomfortable wagon seat to hide the telltale bulge from the others.

Beth, he thought, the memory of her genuinely fond now. Even gentle.

How wide her eyes had flown as she felt that first thrust of his flesh. And how much wider as she recognized the quicker, sharper thrust of his blade.

Too late then to cry out.

Too late then to—

"You bastard! What're you smiling at?"

The voice and a hard cuff to the side of his head snapped him out of his reverie and back to the unpleasant realities of the present.

Dane Florette opened his eyes and looked with kindness

at the bearded, weather-creased face of the sheriff whose fetters he temporarily wore.

"Sorry," he said. "I was woolgathering."

"You son of a bitch," the lawman said. "You ain't fooling anybody with that smug fucking grin of yours. Set there an' act like butter wouldn't melt in your mouth, you bastard. You'll hang from the gallows quick as I get you back."

Florette's eyes grew wide with genuine alarm. Then he calmed when the wagon driver turned and snapped, "Aw, leave him be, John. A young gentleman like this couldn't of—"

"You shut your fucking mouth, Turley. I want your fucking opinion I'll ask for it."

"I just—"

"You'll just shut your fucking mouth, that's what you'll just. This cold-blooded son of a bitch killed that girl."

Florette smiled, his composure recovered now and his erection gone. Under the circumstances, that was just as well. He gave the sheriff a smile that was clear-eyed and genuinely warm. "I know you are having difficulty believing me, sir, and truly I cannot blame you. Or I wouldn't have come with you so willingly. As soon as we reach Olympia and I can contact my attorney, you will realize your error." The smile broadened and became even warmer. "And no harm done, sir. Why, I am as anxious as you to find the true perpetrator of so terrible a crime."

"See?" Turley demanded.

"Did I tell you . . ." the sheriff started in a low, menacing tone.

Turley gave him a look of wounded innocence that did not look half so innocent as the smiling blandness of Dane Florette's expression. "I just don't think we should forget that a guy's innocent till proven guilty, John. That's all."

"Innocent, shit," the sheriff snorted. "I'll tell you how innocent I think this cocksucker is, Turley. I think he's so fucking innocent that if I think some smart-ass lawyer is gonna get him off in front of some halfwit fucking judge and some bleeding-heart fucking jury, I'll take the sonuva-bitch outside an' turn him loose."

Florette blinked. He honestly did not understand what this country bumpkin of a sheriff was getting at. The words themselves were entirely reasonable. Just, in fact, what Florette was counting on arranging. Yet they were spoken with an odd note of threat in them. Florette found that really quite strange.

"I can't believe you'd do that, John."

"By God, I will," the sheriff swore. "You just watch and see if I don't."

"Damn it, John, we haven't had a lynching in . . . I can't remember how long it's been. Since my daddy's time, I guess. Maybe longer."

"We'll by God see one in your lifetime an' mine if anybody thinks he'll put this bastard back where he can harm decent girls again."

Florette felt his gut wrench and a chill race up his spine as the meaning of the sheriff's words became clear. A lynching was . . . unthinkable.

He wanted to shout out his denial. *The cunt deserved what she got. She had to die. It was all justifiable.* But they would not have understood. These fools would have taken explanation for confession. And neither confession nor hanging were a part of his plan.

There was so much *more* he had yet to accomplish.

There was so much more he had yet to do.

"Truly," he said calmly, recovering his composure, "this will all be straightened out as soon as I can wire home and arrange—"

"You'll arrange to say your last prayers," the sheriff snarled. "An' then you'll hang."

"You're upset, John," Turley said in a soothing voice.

"Beth was too close t' you."

Florette blinked again. Smoothly he kept his surprise from showing. But how ever would a well-born young lady like Beth have been close to this . . . this rube with the to-bacco stains on his teeth.

"My condolences, Sheriff. Naturally I had no way to know that the . . . the victim of the horrid crime was known to you personally. And naturally I take no offense at your mistaken treatment of me as your, uh, suspect. I do hope, sir, that you will catch the true criminal and bring him to quick justice."

The sheriff glared at him, refusing to buy any of it. It was Turley who turned in his seat again and explained for Dane's benefit. "The sheriff's daughter Mary an' Miss Beth were best friends, Fogarty."

"Thank you for telling me, sir. It explains much and takes away the sting of this . . . misunderstanding."

"Sure," Turley said agreeably. "You're taking this real Christian, Mr. Fogarty."

Florette was grateful for the information. And for the reminder. They thought of him as a fictitious Doug Fogarty, not as Dane Florette. That was going to make it a trifle difficult when it came time to contact the family and arrange a legal defense. The truth. . . . He set the worry aside. He could think about it later.

"Like I told you," the sheriff said darkly. "You can set there and playact all you want, asshole. We get to town, mister, you're one dead fucker. I seen that poor child's body. Turley didn't. I seen what you done to her. And I know the things that you done and we didn't talk about out o' respect for the poor, dead girl's family. But I know, and you ain't fooling me a lick with your fancy ways an' city manner, asshole. Comes the time we get you back, you'll hang, asshole, if I have to swing the loop myself an' go to jail for it afterward."

The sheriff moved closer and knelt on the swaying, jolting wagon bed so that his reddened, angry face was only inches away from Florette's.

"You're gonna hang, asshole, if it's the last thing I do on this earth," he swore.

Florette felt a coldness in his belly, the cold chill of death. But this time there was no pleasure in the nearness of death. Because this time it was he being sought by the terrible reaper.

The fear brought with it a cold and sure belief that the sheriff intended exactly what he said.

This fool would hang Dane Florette even if he had to violate the law to do it.

Florette became pale from the rush of sudden terror.

For the first time since these idiots had taken him he felt a genuine fear for his own mortality in their hands.

"You hear me, asshole?" the sheriff spat directly into Florette's drawn, haggard face. "You're gonna hang. An' I'm gonna be the one to hang you. One way or t'other, Fogarty. From a gallows or a tree, makes no nevermind to me. 'Cause when you look at me you look at your hang-man, mister."

The sheriff screwed up his face into a scowl and spat, the thin fluid, slightly brownish from the man's last chew, dribbling down over Dane Florette's beardless chin.

"Please. Please," Florette blubbered. "Don't . . ."

He acted as if he wanted to cringe away from the vicious sheriff. His shoulders hunched and he seemed to contract within himself.

Yet instead of moving backward, away from his accuser, he leaned forward.

The sheriff straightened his shoulders and gave the prisoner a triumphant glare.

As he did so Florette's bound hands, tied in front of him by Turley for greater comfort while they traveled, shot forward, fumbling at the sheriff's belt.

"What the . . ."

The sheriff twisted, trying to throw himself backward out of reach.

He was too late.

Florette already had hold of the carved bone grips of the sheriff's .455 Webley revolver.

The gun came free of its holster, remaining in Florette's hands, as the sheriff flung himself backward, sprawling against the back of Turley's seat and nearly spilling the driver off the seat as the sheriff came to rest in a corner of the wagon box with his legs twisted under him.

"No!" the sheriff roared.

He gathered himself, struggling to regain lost balance, as Florette shifted his grip on the bulldog revolver and pointed it.

"What the hell is going on . . ." Turley started, pulling on the reins and turning half around.

He looked in time to see the sheriff come to his hands and knees, then launch himself toward the prisoner.

The revolver in Florette's hands exploded flame and lead, and the heavy slug from the English gun crashed into the sheriff's forehead at point-blank range, singeing the man's face with powder burns and touching off a brief flame in his hair that left a stink behind it in the still air.

The sheriff collapsed onto the wagon bed at Florette's feet, dropped as quickly and cleanly as a shoat under the ax.

For a moment, a few seconds only, the dead sheriff's legs twitched in reflexive spasms, driving dead feet against the slick boards of the floor. Then the body was still, and gases bubbled and rumbled, releasing themselves from a suddenly loose sphincter.

Florette stared at the dead man as if in shock, and Turley sat half turned on his seat and stared as well.

Florette blinked and looked at Turley. "You heard . . . you heard what he said. He would have hanged me. I . . . I can't . . . couldn't . . . allow that. Could I?"

"Oh, Jesus, mister," Turley moaned. "Now what're we gonna do?" He could not take his eyes off John lying there dead on the wagon floor.

"I . . ." Florette blinked again. Then he smiled.

He sat upright and smiled at Turley. In a calm and perfectly reasonable—even a gentle—tone of voice he said, "I suppose I shall have to change my name again, shan't I?"

"What . . . ?"

Florette stood and held both hands forward, pointing the

revolver, clutched awkwardly and unfamiliarly in them, toward Turley's pale, startled face.

"But I never—"

Turley did not have time to finish his protest. The revolved roared for the second time, and a thick, stubby, conical pellet of hard lead ripped into his face, plowing through bone and tissue and snapping what remained of his head backward.

Turley toppled off the driving box and fell onto the spreaders and trace chains, hanging suspended there, his weight startling the horses into motion so that Florette, too, lost his balance and fell out of the wagon.

The driverless horses plunged forward down the road, and Dane Florette picked himself up from the dust and tried to brush off some of the filth that clung to his handsomely tailored clothing.

He was shaken and trembling but unharmed.

He took a few moments to recover his composure and allow his heartbeat to slow to a normal pace, then took a deep breath and felt much better.

He realized he was still holding the revolver in his hands. With an awkward swing of both arms he tossed the gun into the bushes that lined the road here. He did not like guns. Never had. They were loud, brutal, boorish things.

It was really too bad he had not remained in the wagon, he realized. One or both of those dead men would have been carrying a pocket knife at the very least. Better, he might have recovered his own lovely little blade.

Still, the loss of one small knife was small penalty to pay in exchange for his life.

And there would always be some way he could sever the cord that poor fool Turley had used to tie him with.

Smiling now, feeling really quite lighthearted and gay again, Dane Florette left the public roadway and walked off into the forest that stretched for endless miles into the distance. The wagon bearing the bodies of Sheriff John Simmons and county-employed laborer Howard Turley was far up the road by now, out of sight and completely out of mind.

Dane Florette was free and very much at peace with himself.

There was *so* much he wanted yet to do.

CHAPTER TWO

Allan Pinkerton kept Raider waiting in the outer office a good half hour before the summons came to join him and the client inside. That was unusual. But then this was an unusual case if office rumor was correct and Raider really was being asked to pick up on the Manton thing.

The truth of it was that Raider rather resented being considered for the Manton case. Twice in the past year and a half Allan Pinkerton had accepted Eduard Manton's case; each time, the assigned operatives were able to work on the investigation for only a month before Manton's funds ran out. Each time the operatives had come up dry. Word was that the Manton thing would come up dry *every* time for the simple reason that Eduard Manton was a loony whose real need was not so much to catch a criminal as to exorcise a ghost from his own past.

The whole situation had a sour flavor to it among the operatives employed by the Pinkerton National Detective Agency. And as a senior operative—and probably the best in the whole damned agency, too—Raider frankly resented being called in now by Allan Pinkerton and Eduard Manton. While he waited on a cheap, butt-numbing straight-backed chair outside Allan's office, Raider couldn't help wondering if he was beginning to lose favor here in the Chicago headquarters of the famed detective agency. Office politics, perhaps? If that was it, damn it, he would—

"You can go in now."

Raider's thoughts returned from their wanderings, and he joined Allan and Manton.

"Sit doon, lad," Allan said pleasantly enough. He gestured toward the client. "This gentlemun, lad, is Mr. Eduard Manton. Mr. Manton, Raider here is mah vera best operative, just as I told ye."

That made Raider feel a little better. Whether Allan still believed that or not, he was still saying it to the paying customers.

Raider gave Manton a quick once-over when the thin man stood and offered his hand. He had heard much about Manton before, of course, but he had never seen the fellow until now.

There was not much about him that would impress. He was tall enough, but he was painfully thin, his flesh hanging loose at the jowls like that of a man who has recently lost weight from a protracted illness, and there was an unnatural—and unhealthy—brightness in pale eyes sunken behind dark bags. His hair was thinning and dull, and there was a faint, yellowish undertone in his complexion.

Even his clothing contributed to the overall appearance of a man gone quickly to seed. His suit had been tailored for someone larger than the man who wore it now, so that it hung awkwardly from bony shoulders, and the material was scuffed and fraying although clean.

When they shook hands, Manton's grip was limp. He felt almost fragile, Raider thought.

"Pleased to meet you, sir," Raider said politely.

He stood half a head taller than the client and, lean though he was, probably outweighed the man by forty pounds or more. Raider was a study in ominous dark shades. Black hair. Sweep of jet mustache indifferently trimmed. Flashing dark eyes. Craggy, deeply tanned features. The big Remington revolver that rode at his waist even here in civilized Chicago seemed a natural part of his body rather than an appliance strapped there for convenience.

Eduard Manton studied Raider for a moment, then silently nodded and resumed his chair in front of Allan Pinkerton's desk.

"Are ye familiar wi' the gentlemun's case, Raider?"

"Some," Raider admitted.

"Mr. Manton has come into possession o' new facts that he 'ould like us to look into, Raider."

Raider grunted noncommittally. That was the sort of crap that would be said whether it was true or not, by Manton hoping to convince Allan to tackle the case once more, by Allan being polite to the paying clientele. It didn't necessarily mean anything.

Allan nodded to the client, and Manton pulled a worn and dog-eared newspaper clipping from a pocket. He unfolded it with care and leaned forward to hand the bit of paper to Raider, treating the scrap of newsprint almost with reverence.

It took Raider only a moment to review the clipping. He had read a similar version in a local newspaper not five days before, so he was already passingly familiar with what it said.

"What does this have to do with us?" Raider asked.

Again Allan deferred to the client, who said, "It's the same man, Mr. Raider. That is the same man who murdered my Liz."

Raider frowned. "I hate to disappoint you, sir, but I don't believe anyone can be so sure about that. As I understand it, your daughter, was, uh, died in Kansas City. This incident took place in Washington State. Just because in both incidents it was a young girl who died—"

"Please," Manton interrupted. "I am not jousting with windmills, sir."

Raider failed to see what the hell kind of connection that had to do with anything, but he let the sickly client talk on.

"I contacted the authorities in Olympia, Mr. Raider. On a confidential basis, of course. In fact, I went there myself immediately after hearing about the murder of that poor child Beth Armister. I spoke personally with the sheriff whose murder is reported in that article. The . . ." His face twisted, and it took him a moment to recover his composure. "The circumstances . . . the events are markedly simi-

lar to my Liz's murder, Mr. Raider. Miss Armister was
raped as well as murdered."

"But—"

"Please," Manton said quickly. His eyes were bright
with a zealot's conviction, and his voice was that of a man
who would beg if he had to. Raider sat back in his chair
and let the man go on.

"The sheriff confided certain details of the case to me,
Mr. Raider. Details that were not released to the press for
publication for, um, obvious reasons of sensibility. The
family, you understand."

Raider nodded and this time kept his mouth shut. Manton still hadn't said anything that was of interest, but it was
probably best to let him get it out of his system.

"Just as with my Liz, Mr. Raider, the murderer was a
young man the victim met under socially correct circumstances—while participating in a church youth group. This
time the young man called himself Douglas Fogarty. My
daughter was murdered by a man known to us as Dan Fallon. You see the obvious comparison."

Raider nodded. He had to grant Manton that much. Men
using aliases frequently used common initials, as a matter
of fact. It was too thin a thread to build anything on, of
course.

"There is more. The newspaper accounts of the murder
say only that the young lady died from stab wounds."

Again Raider nodded. The stories of the murder had
been circulated several weeks ago, before this later account
of the capture of "Douglas Fogarty" and his murder of the
sheriff and a wagon driver.

"What those accounts did not specify, Mr. Raider, was
that the cause of death was a single stab wound precisely
placed to sever the carotid artery beneath the left ear. And
that, sir, is precisely the same type of wound inflicted . . ."
His voice faltered, then recovered. ". . . on my dear daughter. One stab wound. Almost surgically precise. I have . . .
I have spoken with members of the college of surgeons at
several universities, Mr. Raider. They tell me that death

from rapid blood loss would take several minutes. During that period of time the victim would be conscious, would be aware of her own impending death, would be aware of the other . . . indignities being imposed upon her."

Raider swallowed. Hard. That was damned hard to take. How would it affect the parent of one of those victims was beyond his ability—or desire—to fully comprehend.

"That," Manton went on, "the extreme similarity of the stab wounds, is why I am so thoroughly convinced that this Douglas Fogarty is the same man my . . . my wife and I once knew as Daniel Fallon. I am convinced sir, indeed I *know,* that Fallon and Fogarty are one and the same man. And"—he dug into his pockets again—"I have another clipping here, this one from San Francisco, that makes me suspect yet another victim. A young lady of quality who was murdered, stabbed to death, by an unknown assailant. I tried to learn more about that murder, Mr. Raider, but understandably enough the family would not speak to me about it. By the time I heard of the murder and was able to travel there, the officer who investigated the case had re-signed and moved away. The report he turned in was writ-ten down after the fact by a clerk who had only sketchy verbal accounts to go on. So I can't be sure this third murder is connected, but I believe it at least possible."

Raider felt sorry for the thin, driven man. But damn it, there really was nothing to go on here. The murder had taken place weeks ago. The sheriff and wagon driver were killed over a week past. Even the newspaper story cited authorities who said they believed Douglas Fogarty had escaped by now into British Columbia, where he should be safe from U.S. justice.

"Mr. Manton, I don't know if we could get clearance to make an arrest in Canada even if we could locate this Fo-garty-Fallon fellow." He glanced at Allan for support, but the Scot was carefully examining his fingernails.

"Please," Manton said. "I realize I've made a nuisance of myself. But believe me, I've made a study of this man's methods. He is a beast, an animal, sir. And he'll not stop now. He is a demented creature, and nothing will stop him so long as he is free to prey on innocent girls. When ... when my Lizzie died, Mr. Raider, I was in too much shock ... and my poor wife ..." he shuddered. "This is the closest I've gotten to him since that time. Just a matter of weeks behind him now. And ... you should understand how much this means to me, Mr. Raider. After ... after our Liz was murdered by this fiend, my poor wife could not cope with the pain of it. She has been institutionalized for more than a year now. I ... the business I once had has lapsed. My fault, of course. I ... simply could not bear to concentrate on it any longer. All my resources, everything I have ever had, has gone into this search." The pain lay deep in the man's eyes now as he pleaded with Raider for understanding.

"I realize I wasted the agency's time before. But this time ..." He paused, swallowed, spoke again. "I have money to pay for your services, Mr. Raider. A little. I ... I can sell my home. I'll sell it and pay you a premium over and above the usual agency fees."

Raider glanced uncomfortably toward Allan, whose strict, Scots Presbyterian background never taught him to be scornful of money honestly earned. Allan was still inspecting his fingernails.

"I will do *anything* you ask, sir. Pay you any amount I can raise. But please, please help me bring this monster to an accounting for what he has done." Manton had shifted forward onto the edge of his chair. He was wringing his hands and looked perfectly capable of dropping down onto his knees to beg Raider to help. For one awful moment Raider thought Manton was going to do exactly that.

"You really believe this man has murdered often?"

"I do," Manton said with the simplicity of deep conviction. "I believe he may have murdered very often. And always the innocent. Young girls still in their teens. Maidens with their futures taken from them. Liz was my ... our ... only child. When he killed our Liz, Daniel Fallon destroyed my wife and me as well." Manton's eyes were glistening with unspilled tears that he made no effort to hide.

"Would you mind if I talked to Mr. Pinkerton alone for a few minutes, Mr. Manton?"

"Of course." Manton stood and hurried out of the room.

For the first time in quite a while Allan Pinkerton looked at his best operative. He raised his bushy eyebrows.

"Damn it, Allan, the initials, the stab wounds being the same . . . it just could be this time."

"There's no trail for ye to follow, laddie. The case could be a waste o' the agency's valuable manpower. As it has been twict afore na."

"Goddamn it, Allan, this Douglas Fogarty–Daniel Fallon guy pisses me off. I mean . . ."

Pinkerton looked away as if he were embarrassed. "We've taken tha' poor man's money twict na wi'out success, Raider lad."

"So all right, damn it. We'll do it again. For expenses only, far as I'm concerned. Take it off my vacation time if it comes to that."

Allan Pinkerton coughed delicately into his fist. "That, uh, is what I had in mind, laddie. Except ye'll not lose what free time ye have comin'. An' I'll be payin' yer salary from me own pocket."

Raider grinned. "You phony son of a bitch, trying all these years to prove you never had a heart and then turning up with one anyhow. I'll take the Manton case on one condition. You don't pay me out of your own pocket. We split it. You and me, by damn."

Pinkerton squared his shoulders and nodded. "Done, lad. But by God an' all that's holy, if ye ever tell a livin' soul about this I shall have ye horsewhipped afore I fire ya."

Raider laughed and went to find Eduard Manton and tell the man he had his operative.

CHAPTER THREE

The Western Union office manager smiled and stood politely when he entered the office, and he knew it was all right. The old bastard had come through again. Not that there had ever *really* been any question of it, of course, all the blustering and threats aside. He always did come through. The old man felt guilty, even after all these years, so he always came through in the end.

Dane Florette gave the Western Union employee a cool smile and a nod.

"The draft is here, sir," the man said. "It arrived just a few minutes ago. I was about to send a messenger for you." He had the nervous smile and sticky-sweet demeanor of a serf addressing his better. Florette was used to that, of course. The drab little workman would probably never in his entire life have half so much money of his own in hand at one time. Probably, in fact, would never own a house worth as much.

Dane accepted the draft arranged by his grandfather back east and signed for it. The draft would be drawn against Western Union's accounts anywhere in the country. It was a convenience. It ensured that Dane could make his way in comfort anywhere without the bother of having to go back and actually face the old fossil who was his paternal grandparent.

"Thank you," he said crisply.

The old man had come through, but Dane was feeling a trifle cross. This was the third day since he had sent his wire requesting funds, and his shirt and collar and underthings were all becoming hopelessly limp. Dane Florette did not *like* soiled clothing, and he resented the necessity to wear such now.

He found the nearest bank and cashed the draft immediately, taking all $5,000 in currency. A money belt would have to be among his first purchases.

That business with the stupid sheriff and the wagon driver, whatever their names had been, was unpleasant. He had lost everything when the horses ran off like that, and he did not propose to allow any repeat of the inconvenience.

Not that he really expected to have trouble again. It had only been a momentary flash of poor luck that allowed the sheriff to bother him. It would not happen again. Still and all, a man should be prepared.

He found a suitable haberdashery and outfitted himself with new clothing—it was a pity he had to settle for a suit off the rack, but he didn't want to spend any more time here than was necessary—and bought as well a canvas money belt that fit flat and snug around his lean waist. And of course a folding pen-knife with an inch-long blade. He had lost everything, absolutely everything, to that temporarily lucky sheriff.

Florette still felt affronted that someone of that class had been allowed to bother him.

Why couldn't these people understand the necessity of what he did? It was all perfectly reasonable if only they would make the smallest effort to comprehend.

But then small-minded people like that sheriff never did bother to make that effort.

That was only one of the things that set Dane Florette apart from them. That made him superior to them.

Still, no real harm had been done. It was all behind him now, and he would learn from it.

He paid for his purchases, including a reasonably handsome Gladstone bag to carry it in, and returned to his hotel for another bath and a most welcome change into fresh underthings and a new collar.

He felt much, much better when that was done.

• • •

The passenger train chuffed and bumped to a jerky halt. Dane waited until the aisle was clear before he made his way down onto the platform. A smiling, head-bobbing Oriental porter collected his bag and carried it to a hansom for him.

"Take me to the best hotel in town," Florette ordered.

"That would be the Marchman, sir."

"The Marchman will be fine then."

"Yes, sir." The cab driver touched the brim of his cap and shook the reins to set the horse into motion. "You are a visitor, sir?"

"That's right, but I might stay if I like the investment prospects," Dane said.

"Fine future here, sir. Anyone will tell you that."

"That is what I'm hoping," Dane said. He smiled. "I am definitely looking to the future here."

The hansom passed a tall building of gray quarry stone with old-fashioned flying buttresses built against the side walls and a multicolored round stained-glass window high on the front.

"What would that be?" Florette asked.

"Why, that's the Episcopal church, sir. Very high-toned. The rector is a Father Wirt. Fine gentleman, sir. I've driven him many times."

"The Reverend Wirt, hmm?"

"Yes, sir. I'm sure he would be pleased if you care to attend services come Sunday, sir."

Dane Florette smiled. His whole face lighted up with an open, easygoing joy when he smiled. Everyone who saw him smile invariably found themselves taken with him, and the cab driver was no exception.

"Would you like me to pick you up at the hotel tomorrow morning and drive you to services, sir? It would be a pleasure."

"Yes," Dane mused. "I believe I would like that." His smile became wider and even more winning. "Thank you."

"My pleasure, sir."

It was a five minute drive the rest of the way to the Marchman Hotel. Not terribly close but not too great a walk either. Florette paid close attention to the route the cabby took through the unfamiliar streets. He wanted to be able to find his way back on his own if things appeared suitable there tomorrow morning.

When the cab reached the hotel, Dane Florette was in an exceptionally good humor. He overtipped the driver outrageously, and the man insisted on carrying Dane's bag inside himself, even though the Marchman's doorman could have done it quite as well, and reminded Florette that the cab would call for him promptly at 10:45 the following morning.

"You can't know how much I'm looking forward to that," Dane told him in complete honesty.

"Very good, sir. Tomorrow morning, quarter to eleven." The driver touched his cap brim again and left.

At the desk in the large, ornately furnished lobby of the Marchman, Dane signed the register and casually laid a hundred-dollar bill on the counter to pay for his accommodations in advance.

The bill immediately captured the attention of the desk clerk. Florette's expression did not change in the slightest, but he was vastly amused by the way the clerk nearly turned himself inside out with his anxiety to please.

The fellow snapped his fingers, as quick to lord it over the bellboy as he was to serve this handsome and wealthy young guest.

With a deft twist he spun the register book around so he could read the gentleman's name.

"Escort Mr. Flynn to Suite 4, Benjamin. And see that he is comfortable." To Dane he added with oily deference, "Anything we can do to be of service, Mr. Flynn, anything at all."

Dane smiled at him. "I'm sure I shall be quite comfortable, thank you. I am truly looking forward to my stay here."

The desk clerk bobbed his head eagerly, and the bellman picked up Dane's Gladstone.

The bellman led the way up the curving staircase, and young Mr. Donald Flynn followed.

CHAPTER FOUR

"But Mr. Manton, you just don't understa—"

"Ted," the sickly man corrected gently. "Please call me Ted."

"Okay, sure. Ted. But you just don't realize how difficult a case like this can be. Why, there's no telling what kind of—"

"Raider," Manton interrupted. His smile was just as gentle as it had been—and just as sad—but there was a helpless, hopeless degree of stubborn patience in his eyes that simply could not be denied. "I think perhaps it is you who doesn't understand. You see, Raider, it doesn't honestly matter to me how long or difficult or dangerous this could become. It doesn't even matter that I survive it. So long as Daniel Fallon is brought to justice."

"But you could wait at home, Ted. I'll send you reports. We always have to keep in touch with the home office anyway. I could just send duplicates to you." That was stretching things some, actually. The rules of the agency did indeed say that an operative was to file frequent progress reports, but Raider was well known for his habit of "forgetfulness" when it came to those supposedly mandatory reports. In fact, the Pinkerton Agency frequently heard from him only between cases. This time, though, he was willing to make an exception to his usual patterns.

Manton remained unyielding on the subject. "But you see, Raider, I have nowhere else to go. Nothing else to do. The waiting would only gnaw at me. My business has failed through my own neglect. My wife no longer recognizes me, or anyone else, when I visit her. My . . . I said I would sell my home to finance this venture, and I shall if it becomes necessary. But, uh, what I did not mention before is that while I still own the house, I no longer have the, uh, use of it. I gave it up on a lease. That is how I managed to come up with the cash I have available for the investigation. So really I have nowhere else to go even if I could stand the uncertainty of waiting. I *must* go with you, Raider, or risk becoming as mad as my poor, dear wife is already."

Raider shook his head. How the hell do you argue with somebody like Ted Manton?

It was not something Raider had given particular thought to before, but the Mantons, man and wife, were proof that crime can have more victims than the obvious ones. Their daughter Liz was dead. But she was not the only victim of the man who called himself Daniel Fallon.

Somewhere in Washington State, he was beginning to realize, there would be other parents who were the victims of Douglas Fogarty just as Beth Armister was. The difference was that the girl died. Fogarty or Fallon or whoever the hell he was had sentenced the girl's parents to a living death with the same knife stroke that killed their daughter.

"I'll try not to be a nuisance, Raider. I can't promise to be of any help. I know better than to think that. But I shall certainly promise to be as little burden to you as possible. Anything you say, I shall try to do. Anything, that is, except remain behind."

Damn it, Raider didn't like it. But the poor little simp was so fucking *pathetic* that Raider hadn't the heart to tell him to go away. Kind of like a dog with that just-kicked look in its eyes and its tail tucked down tight. You just don't want to kick that kind away from the fire even if you know you ought to.

Cussing and muttering under his breath, Raider nodded. "All right, Ted. You can come with me. We'll be heading for Olympia on the first train west."

Manton looked so damned grateful Raider was afraid

the man might lick his hand or something. Jeez! That kind of gratitude was embarrassing. "Get your damn bags ready and meet me at the station or I'll be leaving you behind," Raider snapped, suddenly angry—with himself and with Ted Manton, too—and not exactly sure why that was so. "That train oughta leave in an hour or less."

Raider spun on his heels and stalked out of the office without another glance toward the mystified client.

Raider spent most of the trip west grilling Ted Manton about the man he had known as Dan Fallon. The first few efforts were difficult for the dead girl's father. It seemed to become easier for him with practice, particularly after Raider assured him that the information Manton held about Fallon/Fogarty could make all the difference between success and failure in this search for him.

"Yes, of course we knew him," Manton said. "Martha and I were always careful of Liz's friendships. With, uh, boys in particular. She was always such a *good* girl. Never a day of trouble with her. She was always gay and good-natured. Always a joy to us. We . . . had such hopes for her. For her happiness. For the grandchildren we hoped for one day. She was our only child, and we were very proud of her. Very protective."

Information about Liz was not what Raider really wanted, but he knew that the man would have to get this part of it out of his system. Hell, this might be the first time since the girl died that her father was able to really sit down and talk about her with someone. Getting it out now might be good for him, and it wouldn't hurt Raider any. Washington was a long journey from Chicago. They had plenty of time for talk.

"She was only seventeen. But I suppose you knew that." He sighed. "So young. Such a waste. But you were asking me about Daniel. Martha and I met Daniel on several different occasions. We . . . God help us, Raider, we approved of him. He seemed such a *nice* young man. Just a few years older than Liz, I would guess. Handsome young

man with the loveliest smile. Charming, I suppose you
would call him. A blond boy with pale eyes. Always perfect manners, you see. And very well dressed. I would say
that he was most particular about his clothing. Almost
fussy about his appearance."

"A dandy, would you say?"

"Mmm, yes, I think it would be fair to say that. Very
much in the latest style. And generous. He always had
money, and he was free about sharing it. Not stingy at all.
He hosted an ice cream social at the Methodist church.
That is where Liz met him, you see. At the church. Reverend Tyler introduced him to us all, and Daniel hosted a
social for the young people of the church. Martha and I
were among the chaperons for the occasion, and we all met
Daniel that evening. I . . . I've given it a great deal of
thought since, Raider, and I cannot honestly say that I
thought Daniel was paying an unusual amount of attention
to our Liz at the time. No more than he paid to the other
girls or to the boys he met that evening. He was open and
friendly and really quite charming with all the young people, not just with one or two. Martha and I were actually
impressed by him. He seemed so nice, damn his soul to
Hell."

Manton had to stop for a moment to recover his composure. "That was only the first of several occasions. There
was a picnic, too, I recall. We all saw him then. And he
began to attend the youth functions regularly. Liz mentioned that to us. Martha . . . was pleased. I think she har-
bored hopes that Lizzie might strike a match with Daniel
after she graduated school. She hadn't any desire for further education. A life of devotion to a husband would have
suited her so." He had begun to cry, which Raider pretended not to notice, although Manton made no effort to
hide his emotion.

"It was after one of those youth meetings that . . . that
Liz was murdered. A group of the young people were
walking home. All of them together. They weren't paired

off or anything like that. Our Liz was much too young yet to be thinking of such things."

Which was something that a father might blindly believe if it pleased him, Raider thought, saying nothing about it. In his experience, young girls were just as horny and curious as young boys were. They just hid it a hell of a lot better for the sake of appearance and what was expected of them.

"The group got smaller as the youngsters dropped off at their homes until there were only Liz and Daniel and a girl named Mae Dunwiddy remaining. They had long since gone by the street to the hotel were Daniel was staying."

Raider's interest perked up, but he remained silent, not wanting to interfere with Manton's account.

"Mae told the authorities later that Daniel offered to escort the girls on and return to his hotel when they were safely home. She said . . . she said the three of them laughed and played a word game while they walked. Something to do with puns. It was a game and . . . she said our Lizzie was having a gay time in her . . . in her last hours." Manton pulled out a handkerchief and wiped red-rimmed eyes. He took a deep breath and tried again.

"They stayed a while outside Mae's home, the three of them on a swing on her front lawn. They didn't want the game to end. Then they told Mae good night, and Liz gave Mae a kiss on the cheek, and Mae went inside. That was . . . that was the last anyone other than the murderer ever saw my Liz alive, you see."

Raider nodded solemnly and waited.

"Mae's home is only a block and a half from mine . . . ours, I mean. It should have taken them only a moment to get there. Instead . . . we will never know under what pretext—they turned back to the church. I . . . I've guessed that he would have told Liz he left something forgotten at the church. And suggested perhaps that they might continue their game of puns if she walked back with him. It was dark by then, of course. And there are no gaslights in the neighborhood. No one saw them returning to the church. Reverend Tyler had already locked the hall and left. The . . ." His voice broke, and he wiped his eyes again. "The sanctuary was open. It was never locked, you see. He . . . he took her inside there. And . . . and up to the front. Right in front of the altar. And . . . that is where . . . that is where . . ."

"It's all right," Raider said gently. "You don't have to talk about that."

Manton nodded gratefully.

As much now to change the man's train of thought as to gain information, Raider asked, "Did Daniel ever talk about himself? Where he came from? Who his parents were?"

"Why . . . no, I suppose he didn't."

"You said he lived in a hotel. Was he alone?"

"Oh, yes. The police checked that, you understand. The people at the hotel said they couldn't recall him ever receiving any visitors, not even any mail. He was quite alone."

"You said he was generous and that he always had money. Where did he work?"

"Oh, he didn't work. He was only nineteen or twenty, remember."

Raider almost laughed at that one. To Ted Manton that explanation was probably quite reasonable. A young man of means was not expected to support himself until he was good and ready. If ever. Personally, Raider had been making his own way, one way or another, pretty much since he was belt high to a pissant. Still, the information told Raider more about Daniel Fallon than Ted Manton might ever realize.

"He never mentioned his past?"

"Never," Manton said firmly. "Believe me, Raider, I've tried to recall every word I ever heard him speak. There was nothing. I asked Reverend Tyler about that too. Daniel was such a delightful, witty companion that no one particularly noticed the things he did not say about himself. He never once mentioned anything about his personal history to anyone at the church. Or anywhere else so far as we can determine. The home address he gave at the hotel was Cambridge, Massachusetts. The police there report no knowledge of a Daniel Fallon by that name or by description."

"Isn't there a college of some sort there?" Raider asked.

Manton gave him a curious look, then said, "Yes, there is a college of some sort there. The police contacted them. They have no record of a student by that name. As for the physical description, they wouldn't venture an opinion. Probably there have been hundreds of students who were blond and slender and wealthy and charming."

Raider grunted. "The sonuvabitch had to be getting his money from someplace."

"From his parents," Manton agreed. "Whoever they are and wherever they might be."

"Maybe he slipped up and said something around Olympia," Raider suggested, although he was not particularly hopeful about it.

"Do you think so?"

Raider shrugged. "There has to be something we can pin him down with." He grinned. "My job's to find it, Ted. That's what I do. I get onto a bastard like this one an' I dog him until he makes a mistake. An' then I use that mistake to nail his balls to the wall."

"But first he has to make a mistake?"

"He's already proved that he makes mistakes, Ted. He's killed two girls. Maybe more. That right there is a mistake."

Manton gave Raider a wan smile, the first he had been able to manage in quite some time. "It's a pity," he said, "that you were speaking figuratively about that."

"About what?"

The pale man's eyes turned deadly cold. "About nailing Daniel Fallon's testicles to a wall. Now that you've mentioned it, Raider, I believe I would enjoy posting them over my mantel. I really would." Manton turned his head and stared out toward the scenery rolling past the train windows.

Ted Manton's attitude toward a simple figure of speech was probably something that wouldn't get a whole lot of public approval. But Raider couldn't exactly fault the fellow for it. Come to think of it, after seeing the change in those pale, maybe no longer quite so hopeless eyes, Raider wasn't even so sure he would deny that Eduard "Ted" Manton wasn't capable of doing exactly that now that the idea'd been planted.

Raider propped his boots on the seat facing him, tilted his black Stetson forward over his eyes, and tried to get some rest while he could. There was no telling what would be waiting for them in Olympia. All he knew for sure was that he needed some small slip on Fallon/Fogarty's part so Raider could commence the dogging he had gone and half bragged about to Ted Manton. For the sake of Liz Manton's dad and probably that of a bunch of girls Raider would never know or even hear about, he didn't want the Pinkerton Agency to disappoint Manton a third time.

CHAPTER FIVE

Don Flynn leaned closer to the mirror and inspected his face, particularly along the jawline, with critical attention. Don Flynn was twenty years old and had never shaved. Dane Florette, on the other hand, would be twenty-five in another two months and had to work at maintaining Flynn's youthfully beardless appearance.

Florette had never shaved either, but nowadays it was costing him some discomfort to avoid what would all too soon become a necessity. A little downy peach fuzz on his cheeks was a positive blessing that helped him to hold on to his boyish appearance. He managed it by the method he was intent on now: frequent inspection of his face for any hairs that were becoming too coarse or too thick to fit the image he created for himself. Anything beyond the self-imposed limits of acceptability were plucked with tweasers instead of cut. He believed that shaving would only make the beard worse and was willing to accept the pain of tweasing instead.

He found a hair, nearly an inch long and dark enough to be noticeable, and grimaced as he pulled it out. Then he craned his neck, angled his head this way and then that, searching for any more that might deny Don Flynn's stated age. With a grunt of satisfaction he decided he had gotten them all and returned the tweasers to their leather case along with the nail files, cuticle picks, and nail trimmers. Just like Dane Florette, Don Flynn prided himself on proper grooming.

He powdered his underarms, splashed a spicy-scented

lotion on his cheeks and across his chest, and concentrated on dressing.

He felt good, very good, about his opportunities for the future. This morning after worship services, when he introduced himself to Father Wirth—the idiot cab driver had misled him into embarrassment by failing to pronounce the rector's name correctly—it was the preacher—priest? Dane was not sure just what the hell you did call one of these Episcopalians or Anglicans or whatever the fuck they were—who had come up with the suggestion that young Don Flynn attend the youth meeting tonight.

It couldn't have been more perfect. Don hadn't even had to suggest it himself. It was all Wirth's idea. Wonderful.

Don stood in front of the mirror for a moment before he pulled his shirt on. He gave his torso the same closely critical inspection he had just devoted to his face, twisting and turning, absolutely refusing to suck his belly in or resort to any measure of artifice.

Not that he needed to. Not yet. His waist was still as trim as it had been when he was sixteen, and his chest was as hairless as his chin. He could still easily pass for eighteen if he wanted to, but he didn't want to push it that far. Twenty would do.

He smiled. It might be years yet before he had to assume an age that would put him beyond youth groups.

He selected a crisply starched shirt, a brand-new celluloid collar, and a fresh tie and finished dressing. He wanted to be ready in plenty of time to start out early. No cabs this evening. He wanted to walk the two miles to the church and begin getting a feel for the streets and the timing here.

It was suppertime, but Don Flynn was not at all hungry. His growing excitement allowed no room for thoughts of food now.

He fashioned the knot in his tie with great care and picked up a pair of heavy, silver-backed brushes to begin working on his hair.

* * *

"Just for the pleasure of it," Don Flynn answered. "I wasn't concentrating on my grades, you see, so Dad suggested I take a year off from the studies and travel. Get it out of my system was the way he put it." He smiled and touched the young man on the elbow in a companionable gesture. "But really, it's quite boring talking about myself." He laughed. "I know all about me, you see. I'd like to hear more about *you* now that I've had the pleasure of meeting you."

The young man, a solemn and bespectacled boy of eighteen or so, flushed with pleasure at the newcomer's interest in him and began to talk.

Flynn listened with unfeigned attention. There was no artifice in it whatsoever. He genuinely *was* interested in everything Peter Hansen had to tell him. And in whatever any of the other youth group members might say. That was a large part of his charm. Don Flynn preferred to say as little as possible about himself. He listened with complete attention when anyone else spoke. He cared about them. He was never critical or unsympathetic.

He listened every bit as carefully to the acne-stricken and unattractive Peter Hansen as he did to handsome Ralph Urbanek.

He was as polite and charming and attentive with fat Maudie Wayne as he was with vivacious, lash-fluttering Annalee Johnson.

It required a great deal of discipline on Don's part, but he was not even especially attentive to Elizabeth O'Neill, who was standing now by the punch bowl.

He didn't even look her way while he spoke with—listened to was more like it now—the Hansen boy.

But he could feel the glow of anticipation somewhere low in his belly when he happened to catch a glimpse of her.

Like all the others in the small group, the visitor had been introduced to Elizabeth earlier, before the brief Bible study, before the spirited if somewhat discordant hymn-sing, and before the refreshment and social session.

The whole thing was a real pleasure to Don Flynn. In particular, though, the meeting with Elizabeth.

Peter's discourse on his hopes for the future was interrupted by Mrs. Wirth—Don hadn't realized that priests were allowed to marry, a fact which he carefully hid when the introductions were made—and pretty Vivian Murphy latched on to him and led him willingly toward the punch bowl.

He smiled shyly at Elizabeth O'Neill.

She smiled happily back at him and gave him a perkily bold wink before she turned away to talk with Maudie.

Flynn felt a surge of joy spread with a tingle through his loins.

This was going to be *such* a pleasure.

The best ever. He was already sure of it.

Not that Elizabeth was so terribly pretty. Vivian was really much more attractive.

But Elizabeth was special.

During the hymn-sing Don—and he *was* Don now, would be for as long as he remained here—had surreptitiously studied her from the back of the meeting room.

She was sixteen, barely old enough to be a part of this group, and small. Her body, as well as he could judge it under the loose, middy smock she wore, was not yet fully developed. Her breasts were unformed, her hips not yet swelled enough to lend dimension to a waist that was a trifle too wide for the rest of her.

Her brown hair was curled into tight ringlets that were left unbound. The soft ringlets bounced when she moved. Don Flynn found the style quite fetching on her, although normally he preferred blond girls with their hair braided, the braids pinned in tight wraps in the Scandinavian or German style.

Her eyes were blue and very large. Her lips, deliciously pale, were small and thin but mobile, as were her frequently changing expressions.

When he looked at Elizabeth O'Neill's lips it was difficult for him to refrain from imagining those lips, that small

mouth, encircling him, taking him inside the moist heat of
her. With a mouth so small there should be just about room
enough.

Don Flynn—he wondered briefly if he should suggest
they call him Donnie; it sounded younger—accepted the
cup of fruit punch Vivian handed him and listened with
close attention while she told him about the headmistress at
Clara Barkley's School for Young Ladies.

He was honestly interested in what Vivian had to say,
but when Elizabeth and Maudie moved away to join a
small group in conversation on the far side of the room,
Donnie could not help reaching into his trousers pocket
with one hand, sipping from the punch cup with the other,
and lightly touching the shiny new penknife he carried
there.

He was going to have to buy a small whetstone, he
realized. A knife was never truly sharp when it was pur-
chased.

But then, it was a task he would not mind undertaking.
He could sit in complete pleasure for an hour or more,
gently and carefully stroking a whetstone with a tiny sliver
of steel that would give him so much in return for his
attentions to it. Even the feel of the tempered steel sliding
across the fine grit of the stone pleased him, and he was
looking forward to it even as he listened closely to Vivian
relate a story about a classmate's practical joke on two of
the other girls.

Donnie Flynn giggled happily and leaned his head
closer to Vivian's in a conspiracy of shared humor when
she finished her story.

Oh my, Donnie thought, his chest swelling with real joy,
this was a *wonderful* group of young people, and he was
truly glad to become one of them.

Across the room Father Wirth leaned over to whisper
something to his wife, and the two of them smiled indul-
gently at the newcomer who fit in so nicely with the other
boys and girls.

CHAPTER SIX

Raider went through the motions of talking to the police and the acting sheriff in Olympia, but they were not the people he really wanted to see there. The authorities would give him facts, but the facts left behind by Fogarty/Fallon would tell him nothing. It was impressions he needed now. Some hook, some handle that would hint at where the man was now, not where Fogarty once had been.

When he learned that the dead sheriff had wanted control of the investigation because of his own daughter's close relationship with the murder victim, Raider knew who he wanted to see.

"You can come with me this time," he explained to Manton, "but I don't want you thinking that's gonna be a regular thing. It will depend, and I don't want you doing anything to interfere with the investigation. You understand?"

"I think so."

"Good. This time I want you along because that girl has lost her daddy and her best friend to this Douglas Fogarty guy. When she hears you lost a daughter to the same man, she might be willing to talk freer with you than she would with me. But if I get the idea it isn't working that way an' I want you out for some reason, you get the hell outa the way right then. You understand me? No questions, no arguments, you just up an' go if I tell you to. Right?"

Manton nodded. Raider was not sure Manton would actually do it if it came down to it, but at least he had the promise. It was the best he could hope for at the moment.

36

It was a mile and a half to the Simmons house. Normally Raider would have hired transportation to get there, but he was trying to keep Manton's expenses down on this one. They walked the distance, Manton paler than usual and gasping for breath by the time they arrived but not complaining.

Their knock was answered by a large girl in her late teens or early twenties. She wasn't fat, just big: tall and heavy-boned and fleshy without being plump. Raider guessed that Sheriff John Simmons must have been a large man.

He removed his Stetson and nodded. "Miss Mary Simmons?"

"That's right."

The guess was not particularly difficult to arrive at. She was wearing a chocolate brown dress with a band of black velveteen pinned to her sleeve.

Raider introduced himself and Ted Manton. "I'm a detective with the Pinkerton Agency," he told her, "and Mr. Manton is my client. We intend to find the man who murdered your father and Beth Armister, Miss Simmons."

The girl's eyes focused on Manton.

"We have reason to believe that the same man, using a different name, murdered Mr. Manton's daughter Liz in Kansas City two years ago."

"Twenty months ago," Ted Manton corrected. Oddly enough it seemed to be that, perhaps the dull pain in Manton's voice when he said it, that made the difference. Mary Simmons stepped aside and swung the screen door open to allow them inside.

It took a little time and several cups of weak tea before she became comfortable with them.

"I don't want to drag up unpleasant memories, Miss Simmons. We've gotten the bare facts from the police. What I want from you is everything you can tell me about Douglas Fogarty. Everything you can think of, no matter how trivial it might be. Anything might help."

Mary Simmons's expression hardened. "It could help put that son of a bitch on a gallows?"

"That's what we're hoping," Raider said evenly. Mary Simmons, it seemed, was a nice enough girl but not a sheltered child. There was some of her father's steel in her.

"I'll tell you everything I can, then, Mr. Raider." She said it to him but she was mostly watching Manton, wanting the approval of another secondhand victim more than that of a hired investigator. It was what Raider had hoped for.

"Doug was a charmer. One charming SOB. I say that now, but at the time I just thought he was charming. I was actually jealous when Beth told me she thought he was interested in her. Can you believe that? I was jealous."

The poor kid was carrying a burden of guilt, Raider realized, because her prettier and more successful friend had died instead of Mary. He suspected she would be feeling relief because that was so, relief because she was alive while Beth was not, and guilt because she recognized the relief.

Wheels inside of wheels. More victims, in more ways, than ever showed on the surface of things.

"Let me think now. You want to know about Doug," she mused out loud. "He told us he was twenty. I remember that for sure. But now that I think about it he might be older. He looked real young, you understand, but I had kind of a crush on him too, and I guess I paid a lot of attention to him. Now that I think back on it, I can recall that he was getting some wrinkles on his neck. Not so much around the eyes but high on his neck and, like, under his chin. So I think maybe he was really older than he said. Though of course I didn't doubt him at the time."

Raider nodded, wanting to encourage her to continue without interrupting.

"I don't remember that he ever said much about where he came from originally, but I think he'd been in California before he came here. All he really said was that he was traveling. Taking time off from school, I think. He . . . I'm pretty sure he never said exactly what school. But I remember him mentioning Sacramento once. And San Francisco a couple of times. I don't remember exactly what he said about them. Just, like, that he'd been there. Or maybe about a restaurant or church or something at those places. I don't remember for sure."

Raider nodded again. He was remembering Manton's unproven suspicions that Fallon/Fogarty could have been involved in the death of a third girl in San Francisco. He felt Manton stir on the sofa beside him and shushed the man with a quick gesture. He didn't want to get into idle speculations that would distract Mary Simmons.

"He was . . . well, everyone thought he was just wonderful. I mean, he seemed like just about the nicest boy anyone could ever want to meet. Always so polite and sweet. Always really *interested*. I mean he really listened to you. Even to me. I'm not the prettiest girl around, I know that. Beth was pretty. I'm just a big ol' ox of a thing, and if it hadn't been for Daddy's being in politics here I don't suppose I'd've had half the friends I do. But Doug really seemed interested in what I had to say. He acted like he cared about my mind, not just what I looked like. And he was that way with all the kids. He didn't show any favorites. Not really.

"I mean, I couldn't tell that he was interested in Beth. She thought she could, but I never saw it myself. And he was so damned handsome. The son of a bitch. He was so awful handsome. Pretty, almost." She took a deep breath and paused for a moment, although nothing in her expression had given any hint of the emotions that lay behind the mask of her face. This was harder on her than Raider had realized, but he wanted her to keep going as long as she was willing.

"Doug always dressed nice. But not flashy. Right up to the latest styles you see in the magazines. Never anything gaudy. And he was interested in ladies' fashions just as much as in gentlemen's. A girl could talk to Doug about new styles and not feel silly about it. He was really interested. And helpful, too. Trisha Jamison tried a new hair-style once that she saw in a magazine, and Doug noticed how she'd done one little thing wrong—he even knew what magazine she copied it out of—and he helped her get it right so that she looked really pretty. She really did. But he didn't try to get her off alone and kiss her or anything like that. Trisha would have just died if he'd done anything like that, and..." She clamped a hand over her mouth. "Oh, God! I shouldn't've, I shouldn't've said that!" She started to cry, her expression still immobile but huge tears welling out of her eyes and rolling down her cheeks.

It was Manton who leaned forward and placed a com-forting hand over both of hers, which she was wringing together in her lap. "It's all right, Mary. We understand. It was just a figure of speech."

It took her some time, though, to calm down again.

Raider changed the subject to ease her away from that kind of memory. "We understand Doug was always gener-ous. Did you ever know him to work when he was here?"

"No, I guess I didn't. But yes, he was generous. He always had money." She hesitated. "Except once, I think. Give me a minute." With a deep sigh she leaned back in her chair and closed her eyes in concentration. After a mo-ment she straightened. "Yes, I'm almost sure of it. There were some of us who'd gone to a soda parlor after school. We met Doug there, and one of the boys—I don't re-member for sure who it was—was saying something about taking an adventure up onto the peninsula. Up to Mount Olympus. And then we all got to talking about adventures and picnics and such, and Doug...I remember he said he would ask Pastor if he could hire carriages and all of us go on an adventure together. With chaperons and everything, of course. And we were all excited about that and planning for it, and then Doug got kind of quiet and a little bit embarrassed and said he was running low on funds and couldn't do it that weekend like we were talking about. But then the next week, after we'd all almost forgotten about it,

Doug hired two coaches, big ones, and had the hotel pack box lunches for everybody, and we all drove out in the country and had a swell time. And that was . . . that was the last adventure Beth went on with us." She started to cry again.

Raider gave her a moment, then asked, "Do you remember what day of the week it was when you first started talking about this adventure?"

Mary Simmons looked puzzled.

"It could make a difference," Raider assured her.

"How?"

"If we know how long it took him to send for money and get an answer, it might give us some idea how far away his family is. Or his bank. Whatever his source of supply."

"Oh." She straightened again, interested now in the problem Raider's question posed. "I wouldn't have thought of that, Mr. Raider. Let me see now." She thought about it for a moment. "I think . . . I think that might have been on a Thursday. Or it could've been on Wednesday. I'm sure it wasn't Friday, and I don't think it was any earlier in the week. Tuesdays I have a piano lesson, so I never go to the soda shop on Tuesdays. And I'm pretty sure it wasn't a Monday."

Raider smiled at her. "See? That could be a big help. If it was Wednesday, and his real home was close he might be able to send a letter and get an answer by Friday. And all the way across the country would take a lot longer than a week and a half, but you said he had money for the coach hire by the following weekend. That could be a big help, Mary."

"Good. I hope so. I really do. Daddy . . . Beth . . . I miss them so much." She broke down again, and Manton shifted to the arm of the chair she was sitting in. He put an arm around her broad, fleshy shoulders and held her, rocking her gently from side to side.

Raider looked away. The two of them, young Mary

Simmons and pale, sickly Ted Manton, had gone to a place where he could not follow. The two of them shared a grief that was not his, no matter how much he cared about finding the bastard who called himself Doug Fogarty or Dan Fallon or whatever else.

CHAPTER SEVEN

"Your turn, Peter." Donnie Flynn stood, his back and shoulders aching, and relinquished the crank of the ice cream churn to Peter Hansen. Ralph and Albert and a burly youngster named Paul were standing by for their turns again. The boys had been grinding the crank steadily for some time now, and the mixture of sweetened cream was thickening inside its nest of ice so that the handle was becoming difficult to turn now.

Father Wirth was sitting in the shade of a huge tree with a book and a pipe, paying no attention to the young people on their outing.

The girls were gathered near the plank tables where they had already laid out a picnic lunch. They would not eat until the ice cream, that most special treat of all, was finished and packed in ice under a blanket to harden while the crowd ate.

Peter was already starting to sweat from the exertions of the cranking. Donnie gave him a wink of encouragement and loosened his necktie. Some of the other boys were in their shirtsleeves, but Donnie kept his suit coat on. He considered it improper to be seen without it in polite company.

Ralph Urbanek edged closer to Donnie and nudged him with an elbow. Leaning near he whispered, "A couple of us are going to visit a certain, um, house of easy virtue, Don. Tonight, eh? After supper. We'll meet in the square and all go over together. You seem a right guy, see, and I thought, I mean . . . we thought you might want to come along." The

43

corners of his lips twisted, turning his smile into a suggestive leer, and again he nudged Donnie lightly with his elbow.

Donnie Flynn stiffened, his shoulders squared and chin rising high. He gave Urbanek a cold glare.

"L-look," Ralph stammered, "I, uh, I didn't mean to offend you or—"

"You have offended me," Donnie said, his voice every bit as cold as his stare. Nor did he bother to keep that chilly tone low. He spoke harshly and rather loud so that the other boys around them began to look. Even Father Wirth glanced up from his reading to see what the disturbance was.

The Urbanek boy blushed and tried to withdraw, but Donnie followed, forcing an issue of it.

"Don't come around me with your lewd suggestions, Urbanek. Do you hear me? Never again." Flynn's chin rose even higher in haughty disdain, and he looked down his nose at the offender. "Unlike some here, sir, I happen to have been taught better than that. And I shall thank you to keep your distance from me in the future, Mr. Urbanek."

Ralph's coloring deepened to a brighter red, and he turned away to hurry down toward the stream.

The other boys crowded closer, each of them trying at once to ask Donnie what the trouble was, what it was that Ralph had said to prompt so stern a response, but Donnie refused to tell them.

"Never mind," was all he would say on the subject. "I shan't repeat such as that."

Father Wirth moved closer and listened only for a moment to ascertain that no gossip was being passed here, then he followed Ralph out of the grove and in the distance could be seen walking alongside the embarrassed boy, occasionally reaching out to touch Ralph's elbow or shoulder in small gestures of comfort and understanding. Whatever it was the two of them talked about there out of the hearing of the other young people was never spoken of afterward by either the preacher or the distraught young man.

Donnie, meanwhile, had become something of a hero to the rest of the group. Not only for his refusal to participate in whatever it was that Ralph Urbanek had suggested but even the more so for his refusal to discuss it afterward.

Donnie Flynn was quickly developing the reputation of a staunchly decent and thoroughly gentlemanly young man.

Don Flynn, stripped to his smallclothes in the locked and bolted privacy of his hotel suite, was able to relax for the first time in hours. He felt drained by the emotional stresses of maintaining his facade. But he was satisfied, too. The day could not have gone any better. Particularly that business with the Urbanek boy. The idea of what had been suggested was loathsome, but it had turned out to be useful enough.

He pulled an armchair closer to the bed and slumped into it, propping his feet on the edge of the bed. When he looked down at his belly he saw a small, inch-wide fold of flesh where his waist creased, and he frowned. He was getting to an age, he realized, when he would have to begin thinking twice about second helpings at ice cream socials. Flab and youthfulness were not compatible. He was going to have to start doing some sitting-up exercises. And this was twice now this week that he had had to pluck coarse hairs from his beard. Another few years, call it three at the most, and he would have to invent a new ploy; he would not be able to remain a participant in youth groups forever.

With a sigh he reached for his whetstone and fished the tiny penknife out of his trousers pocket, then draped the pants back over the foot of his bed and settled into the chair again with the knife and stone in his lap.

Perhaps, he thought idly, he could present himself as a divinity student.

That had possibilities.

He could be a student but, say, be traveling. On a sabbatical, perhaps. Seeking experience toward a calling to a youth ministry.

He smiled. He liked the sound of that. It should work nicely.

No need for it immediately, of course. But the day would come, and Dane Florette liked always to be prepared for the future.

There were *such* wonderful prospects in his future. Boundless opportunities available to him.

He picked up the knife, opened it, and began stroking the small blade slowly back and forth across the Arkansas stone, using a light pressure and being exceptionally careful of the angle between the blade and the stone. It was the angle that was critical.

He paused every now and then to test the edge against the ball of his thumb, and each time he stopped he took an extra moment to fondle the handle and the blade of the little knife. So small it was but so very lovely. Utilitarian, it was. Its simplicity was elegant. The feel of it pleased him immensely.

In the privacy of his suite he could relax fully, and as he felt the tiny knife he gave himself over to imagination and anticipation, smiling as he did so.

Annalee Johnson was by far the prettiest girl in this group, and she had already hinted on more than one occasion that she would be willing to walk out with him.

Donnie Flynn frowned, wondering if Annalee Johnson had a tartish streak in her. That was despicable if true. He could . . .

He shook his head firmly.

He had other things to accomplish. That did not include random punishment of the obscene.

No, his mission had only to do with Elizabeth O'Neill.

He allowed himself to think of her now, only of her, pushing pretty Annalee out of mind completely.

Elizabeth.

Her pretty friend was flirtatious and quite possibly fast,

but Elizabeth was the hidden Jezebel. The traitorous Delilah, damn her.

The retribution, the delivery, were hers, damn her.

He would do what was right and proper, and it would give him *such* pleasure. Such joy.

He could feel his chest swell at the thought.

With a laugh of delight he realized that he could feel another swelling as well as he allowed himself the pleasure of imagining how it would be with Elizabeth.

She was surely virginal. She would be tight. So very tight. The penetration would chafe him, rub him raw. Dane Florette never minded that. The pain of it while he healed was always a reminder to him of the pleasure that had been. And of the rightness of the thing that gave him both that pleasure and that pain.

He would take extra time with this Elizabeth. Extra time to explore that small, intriguing mouth. To penetrate those mobile lips. To see her forced to shed her pretenses and prove herself the harlot she truly was.

That was the gift Dane had been given. To expose Elizabeth as Jezebel. To expose and to punish.

A low groan escaped Donnie Flynn's lips as he thought about how it would be with Elizabeth.

He tossed the knife and whetstone aside and reached down to his lap, fumbling cloth aside to release an erection that was raging for freedom. For satisfaction.

Firmly, almost brutally, he began to stroke himself, knowing even as he did so that this measure would be only temporary. It would give him only momentary relief. Only enough to allow him to continue in his mission undetected.

The true relief would come only when he brought the Jezebel to her punishment.

Dane Florette closed his eyes and threw his head back, arching his hips out of the chair and straining up and forward as he pounded his own flesh into submission, faster and harder and faster still, until with a moan he spent himself and collapsed in a shallow faint in the empty, locked privacy of the hotel room.

CHAPTER EIGHT

"Raider, I've been thinking."

"Mmmm?" Raider speared a chunk of steak with his fork, then paused to look across the table at Ted Manton.

"What you were saying to Mary Simmons about this killer having to send for money when he runs short."

Raider shrugged. "Made sense to me. Maybe it doesn't to you."

"No, no," Manton said quickly. "It does make sense to me. But perhaps not in the way you were thinking, that's all."

"How's that, Ted?"

Manton looked apologetic. "I realize you are the trained detective here, Raider. But, uh, perhaps I've had more experience than you with business and, uh, finance." He paused, obviously waiting for permission to go on, which Raider gave with a nod.

"After all, Raider, I wasn't always as poor as you find me now. Before . . . before my Liz died, I was quite respected in my field. And quite successful at it too, if I do say so myself."

"You had bucks," Raider said succinctly.

"In short, yes," Manton said with a small smile. "So I've had some experience moving fairly considerable sums of money about, don't you see."

"You still haven't got to the point," Raider reminded him.

"Yes, well, my point is this. You are considering how long it would take for mail to travel from Olympia to wherever the killer's home base is and then back again, is that correct?"

"Uh huh." Raider took a bite of his steak before it got too cold and chewed while he listened.

"The thing is, Raider, no sensible businessman would trust any substantial sum to the mails. Not only for reasons of speed, you see, but of security. Letters and parcels are too easily lost to theft or accident. They can be misdirected and not turn up for months, even for years. True?"

"True," Raider admitted. He chuckled and added, "Once I was sent a . . . well, you could say it was a kinda compromising sort o' note . . . from a lady, if you know what I mean. That gal sure had some interesting things to say, and I sure wished I'd got the thing sooner. But the letter got mislaid somehow an' wasn't delivered until near two years after the postmark on the outside. By the time I got the damn thing an' went to tap on her window like she'd told me to, she was married an' had a kid on the way." He smiled. "She got kinda a laugh out of it an' thought everything turned out okay in the long run. Me, I was wishing the damn people at the post office hadn't been so sloppy. Never did get close to that one, but I sure woulda liked to."

Manton laughed and said, "That is my point exactly, Raider."

"So how the hell are you gonna send money from one place to another if it isn't through the mail?" Raider asked.

"There are two normal methods," Manton explained. "One is by bank draft, which can either be carried by the traveler who sees a need to replenish his funds en route or can be mailed, which necessarily introduces the problems of postal service again. The second method would be by wire. A person can deposit a draft with a Western Union office anywhere and send a draft authorization to any other Western Union office. *Any* other, anyplace in the country." Manton smiled.

"You act like you think that one has to be the way our killer is doing it," Raider observed.

"Indeed I do," Manton said firmly. "And I'll tell you why. If the murderer was already carrying a demand draft that could be posted against his account by other banks, he wouldn't have had to wait for his funds when Mary said he did. This was no later in the week than Thursday, remember. The local banks here in Olympia would have been open on Friday. If he had a demand draft in his pocket already, he could have gone to any convenient bank on Friday and drawn cash against his draft."

Raider grinned. "Good for you, Ted. I shoulda thought of that myself."

"But your background is not one of business. That is where I have the edge on you. And as I said, a draft sent by mail is subject to loss almost as readily as cash would be."

"So you think the guy uses the telegraph whenever he wants money."

"Yes. Although frankly, Raider, a person of wealth would be more likely to carry a draft than seek a new one each time he needs money."

"Unless," Raider speculated, "it isn't *his* account that's being drawn against."

"Now I'm the one whose lack of previous experience is showing," Manton admitted. "Run that one by me again."

"What I'm saying is that this killer is young. Mary Simmons said she doesn't think he's quite as young as he claims, but he's a young enough fella to make himself a member of youth groups—for some reason at churches, but we won't try and get into that right now. The point is, he's still pretty young. It could be that it's his daddy's money he's counting on for his finances. And Daddy, whoever and wherever he might be, isn't giving Junior a free hand with Daddy's bank account. For whatever reason, he doesn't want to give him an open draft. So every time ol' Junior wants money, he has to get in touch with Daddy and ask for it again."

Manton pondered that, then slowly nodded. "Yes. That makes sense."

"Damn right it does," Raider said. "It fits what you say about moving money around over long distances, and it fits what I'd suspect about the killer too."

"It works," Manton said.

"Another thing." Raider added. "Remember this morning when we were talking to the acting sheriff? The fella that took over after John Simmons got killed?"

"Yes."

"Well, one o' the things in that file he showed us was a list of the stuff that was in Simmons's coat pockets when the body was found. The stuff that they figure Simmons must've taken out of the killer's pockets after he was captured."

Manton shook his head. He didn't recall the list. It was another expression of the differences between his background and Raider's.

"If I'm remembering correctly," Raider said, sure that he was, "the stuff that they were pretty sure wasn't John Simmons's an' probably had belonged to the killer included a silk handkerchief, a brass medallion that might've been some sort of good-luck piece, a folding penknife with a blade one and a sixteenth inches, loose pocket change amounting to something like six, seven dollars"—Raider smiled—"and a wallet holding just over twelve hundred dollars in currency."

"So you think . . ."

"So I think the killer was broke again when he got away from Simmons and that wagon driver. Remember, they said those horses were sweated bad when they found the rig all tangled up in a willow thicket. I'm betting that after the murderer shot Simmons and Howard Turley, the wagon run off from him. Otherwise he'd've taken his things back. He's one cool son of a bitch. I think he'd have taken the time to get his wallet and things if he could. So he might've had to send home to Daddy again right after he killed the sheriff."

"That means he would have sent at least one wire home from Olympia when Mary said he ran low on funds and another from some other town after he escaped." ·

Raider nodded.

"We don't know what other town that might have been, though."

"No," Raider said with a grin. "But Western Union could find out. They keep records."

"You think they would cooperate?"

"I *know* we can ask them. And the Pinkerton Agency is on good terms with Western Union. We've done a good bit of work for them now an' then. If the boys out here don't want to peep, I can always ask Allan to give their bosses a nudge."

Ted Manton began to look excited.

"Now don't be setting too much store by this," Raider cautioned. "It's all guesswork so far. Remember, there wasn't anything on that list about the killer's luggage. You know he'd've had luggage with him. He might've got that off the wagon with him, and he could've had a stash of currency there, too. Or it could be that the luggage got left wherever it was that Sheriff Simmons caught up with him an' took him into custody. With nobody left alive out of that wagon except the killer himself, there's nobody who knows where or how Simmons caught the man. Far as I know, nobody's thought to look."

"But we will?" Manton asked, his excitement undiminished despite Raider's warning.

"Damn right we will. After we talk to Western Union and see what they can tell us."

Manton looked eager for the chase now. Ready to abandon his meal and begin at once.

"Calm down, Ted," Raider said. "We won't be able to talk to the Western Union office manager until morning anyhow. It can wait till then."

"But this is the first break—"

"Now damn it, Ted, we don't know yet if it is a break. It's just a possibility. Remains t' be seen if it will turn into something."

"I know it will, Raider," Manton said with feeling. "I just know that it will."

Raider hated to disappoint the pale, trembling man, but the blunt truth was that more leads proved to be blind trails than turned out to be useful.

Still, this was the best they had to go on right now. They would follow the trail as far as it took them, wherever that might be.

CHAPTER NINE

Raider introduced himself and showed his Pinkerton identification to the Western Union office manager. A gilt sign
on the frosted glass of his door said he was H.W. Hargreve.

"What can I do for you, Mr. Raider?" Hargreve asked
without rising to offer a handshake. He acted as though he
wasn't particularly impressed by the Pinkerton's credentials.

"I need some information from you, Mr. Hargreve. I
need to see your records of bank draft transfers for the, oh,
for the past two months. Three possibly. I can't be sure
until I get into them."

Hargreve pushed his glasses down on his nose so he
could peer at Raider through the upper half of the bifocals.
"You wish to see my records? Is that right? Did I hear you
correctly?"

This was not going especially well, Raider saw. He tried
pouring a little oil onto the ruffled waters that were building in Hargreve's attitude by saying, "The agency has reason to believe that a murderer, the murderer in fact of your
own sheriff and Miss Beth Armister, used Western Union's
services to finance his travels, Mr. Hargreve. And the Pinkerton Agency has always had an excellent relationship
with Western Union. I was hoping—"

"Do you have a court order, Mr. Raider?" Hargreve
butted in.

"No, I don't have a court order, but—"

"Unthinkable," Hargreve declared without waiting for

him to finish. "My records are completely confidential. The banks in Olympia and for several towns nearby conduct business—confidential business, I might add—through this office. As do a number of our leading merchants, the stock brokerage . . . why, the list is exhaustive. The best people of this entire area rely on the confidentiality of—"

"Mr. Hargreve," Raider said impatiently, "I need those records to identify a killer. A murderer. Surely you can understand—"

"I can understand this," Hargreve snapped. "You shall have no access to my records until or unless you produce a court order requiring me to comply with your request. Now I bid you good day, sir."

Raider tried to protest, but Hargreve left his desk for the first time and stalked out of his own office to forcibly terminate the interview.

Damn the man! Raider thought with disgust as he jammed his Stetson back onto his head and marched out of the office.

By the time he got out into the lobby where the everyday business was conducted, there was no sign of Hargreve. The man might have gone outside or slipped away through a back door.

Damn him, Raider thought again.

Still, all wasn't necessarily lost. It would just take longer this way.

They had too little to go on as yet to approach a judge with a request for a court order, he knew, but there was always the Chicago headquarters of the Pinkerton National Detective Agency to fall back on.

Damned if he was going to let that asshole Hargreve know what he was requesting, though. Before he sent his message he would encode the thing. He didn't want to give the supercilious Hargreve time to block Raider's request at Western Union headquarters before Allan could get into it.

The code book carried by Pinkerton operatives was in a false bottom in his luggage, and that was back at the hotel.

Good thing Raider had left Manton asleep there this morning, Raider thought as he hurried back to the hotel. The little man probably would have made matters worse if he'd been along to see the way Hargreve acted.

Ted Manton didn't look like much, but Raider was coming to understand that the scrawny man was driven by his quest to find his daughter's killer. There was no telling what reaction he might have to anyone whose stupidity placed a roadblock between the father and the murderer. The little guy might even get violent, Raider suspected.

Not that Raider could blame him for that, but he didn't want it to happen at a time or in such a way that it could interfere with the investigation.

And antagonizing H. W. Hargreve unnecessarily wasn't likely to help matters any.

Raider returned to the room he was sharing with Manton for purposes of economy and found the pale client shaving at the cracked mirror the hotel provided.

"Where've you been so early?" Manton asked, skewing his jaw to the side while he dragged the edge of the razor lightly over his skin.

"Over to Western Union," Raider admitted. He thought about lying, but that wouldn't work. Manton would know something was up when they failed to go to the telegraph office after breakfast.

Manton turned, his expression eager.

"Don't get your hopes up, Ted. I have to send a message to Chicago."

"But—"

"Huh uh. We won't start any fights we can't win. We'll get Allan onto it, and then we *will* win." This time he could only hope that he wasn't lying. Raider really didn't know how much influence Allan could call on with the Western Union bosses.

"But I thought—"

"Just finish shaving. I'll get my message off, then we'll find ourselves some breakfast."

Manton nodded, but he didn't look happy about it.

Raider got the code book from his bag and perched on the foot of the bed to compose his lengthy message—Allan was going to shit when he saw the bill for this one—and transposed it from plain language into the Pinkertons' private code.

"Ready when you are, Ted."

Manton had finished shaving by then and was buttoning his shirt. He still looked upset but at least was keeping quiet about it.

They went first to the Western Union office, where Raider got the wire off to Chicago. There was no sign of Hargreve. The door to his private office was closed, which was probably just as well. Raider really did not want Hargreve and Manton coming face to face just now.

"This will go out soon?" Raider asked politely when he handed the coded message across to the clerk.

"Twenty, thirty minutes it should be on its way," the clerk assured him. The man did not comment on the fact that the jumble of letters made no apparent sense. But then there were probably a fair number of businesses that preferred to have their dealings kept secret too. The Pinkerton Agency was not the only outfit capable of devising a code for the transmission of important information over semi-public wires. After all, anyone with a key and a knowledge of telegraphy could tap onto a wire and listen to whatever traffic was sent.

"Thanks."

"Don't you think..." Manton began, but Raider took him firmly by the elbow and guided him outside.

Once they were on the street Raider said, "It will be tomorrow before we get our authorization, Ted. That's at the earliest. Could be two or three days."

"But..."

"In the meantime, we aren't going to sit here and twiddle our thumbs. While we're waiting to hear from Chicago we'll hire some horses and see if we can't find out if our killer got away with his luggage or if somebody knows something about him wherever he went from here."

Manton nodded, apparently satisfied that they were still actively in pursuit of his daughter's killer. "One thing, Raider," he said.

"Mmmm?"

"Could we hire a buggy instead of a horse? I, uh, I've never learned to ride, actually."

Raider smiled at the thin but plucky little man. "Yeah, Ted, we can hire us a rig instead. Right after breakfast."

Manton grunted with grim determination and led the way toward a cheap cafe they had used before.

CHAPTER TEN

Donnie Flynn's heartbeat had quickened. Every sense seemed more alive, more acute than ever before.

The scent of dust from the streets was sharp in his nostrils, and the evening air felt cool and liquid against his skin. He could hear the sound of an infant crying in a house on the next block, and the slats of the park bench pressed against his back so that he could almost swear he felt the splintery grain of the wood.

He was eager. Expectant. Totally alive in each and every nerve ending.

It was wonderful. This was what he lived for. This was his purpose.

The joy of it flooded through him, sending shivers of pleasure through his body, the flow of it spreading warmth that collected and concentrated in a tingling glow deep inside his groin. Marvelous!

This was Thursday. Every Thursday evening Elizabeth and Maudie met at Annalee's house. Donnie had no idea what they did there. They usually stayed an hour to an hour and a half. They were there now. He had watched them go in, then withdrew to the already located park bench. From here he could watch the street corner where they would soon reappear.

Annalee would remain at her own home, and Elizabeth would walk with Maudie to her house. Then Elizabeth would walk the rest of the way home by herself. It was perfect.

Donnie waited with growing impatience.

There!

Elizabeth and Maudie. Sauntering along together in the twilight. Walking toward fat Maudie's house.

Scarcely able to breathe from the excitement of it, Donnie leapt from the bench where he had been waiting and set off at a quick, purposeful stride, three blocks parallel to the street where Elizabeth and Maudie were walking and at a much quicker pace so he could get well ahead of them. Then over two blocks and down another.

His heart was racing.

The girls were out of sight. But he was sure of where they were at every moment. Was sure of each house they passed and every pause they made. He could see it clearly in his mind, as completely as if he were hovering silent and invisible above them to watch as they moved.

Elizabeth would be saying goodbye to Maudie now. The two would be lingering at the foot of the path from the street to Maudie's front door. Donnie smiled and leaned against the rough bark of a tree that shaded the street in the next block down from Elizabeth's house.

He timed it, concentrating hard on the imagined actions of the unseen girl, and at exactly the proper moment stepped out onto the narrow footpath that ran alongside the street here like a sidewalk in an older, more civilized community.

Perfect!

He was no more than just in motion, idling along with a light, whistled tune on his lips, when Elizabeth turned the corner two blocks away and came toward him.

Donnie wore no hat. He seldom did, thinking a bowler or derby tended to make him look older. But he touched his forehead and smiled when Elizabeth drew near in the middle of the next block.

He smiled at her, his charm boyish and innocently disarming.

"Miss Elizabeth. How nice that I've run into you."

She stopped and smiled back at him. She was so slight

of stature that she had to tip her head back to look up at him. "Mr. Flynn. Good evening."

"I intended to call on you later if it wasn't too late," he said. "This meeting saves me a trip."

"Oh?"

"I was talking with Father Wirth just this afternoon. About forming a youth choir. Separate from the regular choir, you understand. He said he thought the youth choir might sing at worship services one Sabbath each month. And your name came up. I took the liberty of suggesting you as director," Donnie said easily.

"Oh, but I couldn't." Elizabeth blushed delicately and lowered her eyes.

"You're being modest," Donnie pressed. "I've stood near you during the Sunday-evening sings, you know. You have a wonderful voice."

"You're just saying that, Mr. Flynn."

"Not at all. But if you don't want to lead, surely you would be willing to help organize the group." He laughed and winked at her. *Bitch. Jezebel.* He smiled.

"Of course I would be glad to help any way I could," she said, flattered, pleased to have been asked, not really willing now to drop the idea that she should be chosen to lead the group.

"I have an idea," Donnie said with cheerful eagerness. "I'm on my way over to the church now. To meet Father Wirth there and discuss the idea more. Couldn't you come with me and hear what he has to say about it? Please?" He laughed again. "I warn you, though, he and I shall try our best to persuade you."

"I don't know. . . ."

"Please?"

Elizabeth relented. He knew she would. He counted on it.

"All right."

Laughing, truly excited now, he offered the girl his arm, and they walked together toward the church.

It wasn't far.

And by now it was fully dark, the twilight of the evening fading.

No one was likely to notice them together. Even if someone did there would be no harm done. Elizabeth would not be missed until later tonight. She would not likely be found until sometime tomorrow. By then Donnie Flynn would be long gone. He would not even exist any longer.

Donnie smiled but refrained from giving Elizabeth's tiny waist an affectionate hug as he wanted to. It was still just a bit early for that. But soon. Oh, so very soon.

Her fingers rested lightly on the crook of his elbow, and she walked beside him the few blocks to the darkened church.

Elizabeth talked while they walked. She and Maudie and Annalee were planning a surprise for everyone. She teased but would not say what it was. It was something Donnie would like.

That was fair enough. Donnie had his secret too about what it was he would like.

"There aren't any lights on," she said as they came close to the church. "Didn't you say—"

"He told me he'd be in the basement. Going through old records or something like that. I don't remember. He said to come around back and go down the cellar steps."

"Oh."

"I hope you know the way. I've never been down there before," Donnie lied.

"Sure. I'll show you." She slipped her hand off his elbow and took his hand to lead him off the path and across the churchyard. A low stone wall formed a sort of courtyard at the back of the church. Elizabeth led him through the sagging gate and on to the storm cellar doors that Donnie had opened earlier in the afternoon.

"I see the lamp now," she said. "Watch your step and stay close behind me."

"All right." He hoped the words sounded natural to her.

There was a lump growing in his throat that felt as if it would choke him.

Elizabeth stepped carefully down the uneven stone stairs and ducked her head to enter the basement through the storm cellar doors. Donnie lagged behind for a moment and quietly eased the doors closed. Not that anyone was likely to hear, of course, but it never hurt to be cautious.

"Father? Pastor?" Elizabeth led the way, ducking to clear the floor joists overhead even though she was much too short to bump into them.

The lamp Donnie had left burning in the basement earlier was past the coal bin in a large, damp storage area littered with old oddments of broken furniture and the decorations left behind by a generation of Christmas plays and Easter pageants.

"Father?"

Puzzled but not yet alarmed, Elizabeth turned to give Donnie an inquiring look and a shrug. "He must have stepped out for a minute."

"Perhaps," Donnie said smoothly.

He stepped up in front of the girl and looked down at her closely. Inspecting—memorizing for all time—every curve and line and texture of her face.

Her skin was flawless. Her eyes were large. Wondering. Still trusting.

Donnie began to laugh again.

He lifted his hand and gently ran the ball of his thumb along her cheek and across her jaw.

Elizabeth blinked, confusion and the first nagging inklings of doubt beginning to be reflected in the depths of those blue, wide eyes.

"M-Mr. Flynn?"

Donnie smiled at her.

This time the smile was true. At this moment he felt a serenity that extended all about him, encompassing Elizabeth with a warm and gentle love.

In spite of the wickedness of Elizabeth's nature, he was

going to save her from herself. He would bring her to retribution and through retribution to salvation.

The pleasure he derived from this, he believed, had
mostly to do with the saving of Elizabeth from herself.

He would do this *for* her. He would do this for Elizabeth, not for himself. And this, this bringing her back from
the jaws of sin through the repayment with momentary
pain, was the truest expression of love any boy could ever
hope to give any girl.

He wondered sometimes if his efforts were ever appre-
ciated by the girls he saved from themselves.

Someday later they would be able to tell him for themselves.

He was sure they would be grateful to him.

Donnie cupped Elizabeth's cheek in the palm of his
hand. He leaned down and gently brushed her lips with his.
She stiffened but did not pull away.

He could feel her lips—those lips he had thought and
dreamed so much about—tremble at his touch. Her breath
was coming faster now. He could feel it light and warm
against his skin.

Elizabeth sobbed quietly but opened her lips to his when
he kissed her the second time.

"I didn't . . . I never . . ."

"I know," he whispered lovingly.

He pulled her closer, and she kissed him with a touch-
ingly awkward fervor.

How strange that the Delilah, the whore, should be so
inexperienced.

Donnie sometimes wondered about that. Yet it was so.

His chest grew full with the knowledge of what he could
do for her, and his hand tightened its grip, sliding from her
cheek to the back of her neck and clamping firm on the
slender column of female flesh.

Elizabeth's eyes opened wide, and she tried to pull
away, struggling now and alarmed.

Donnie grabbed her by the throat and shoved, pushing

her backward and pinning her against the rock wall of the dank cellar.

Elizabeth squeaked, too shocked and frightened to cry out.

Donnie held her throat with his left hand and with his right slapped her. Hard. Back and forth, again and again until tears and mucus streamed down her face.

Her hands flailed back and forth, trying to hit him, trying to force him away, but he squeezed her throat harder so that she could not breathe.

"Hold still, you cunt," he hissed.

When that did not work he doubled a fist and punched her in the belly. She sagged and would have fallen except for his grip on her throat.

Elizabeth was in a state of terror now. Exactly as she should be. The terror would drive out conscious thought. It would drive out wickedness. It was what she deserved but also what she needed for her ultimate salvation.

Donnie grabbed hold of the neck of her dress and pulled. A preternatural strength he normally did not possess let him shred the cloth and tear it away from her. He yanked twice more and the dress fell away.

She wore a cotton chemise and baggy cotton drawers. One pull and the chemise lay on the floor. Two and the drawers were gone, leaving her wearing only her dark stockings and high-buttoned shoes.

Her pubic hair was scant and pale. Her breasts were little. Small saucers of soft flesh with tiny rosebud nipples shrunken at their tips.

Dane grabbed her left breast and squeezed, bearing down with all his force, and Elizabeth cried out and arched her back, struggling against the pain of it.

"Bitch. Whore." His voice was accusing but controlled. Low and calm and vicious. "Cunt."

He squeezed again, one breast and then the other, his nails biting into her and leaving livid marks behind.

Elizabeth tried to speak, to cry out to him, but she could not.

"I know you, Jezebel," he accused.

He shifted his left hand, letting go of her throat and taking a fistful of the soft, curling hair he had so admired since that first night he met her.

He flung her down onto the earthen floor. Onto her knees at his feet.

Fumbling, anxious, he undid the buttons of his fly. His rigid, throbbing member pointed into her face.

He pulled forward on the back of her head, forcing her onto him, forcing himself into that tight, small mouth, past those pale, tremulous lips.

Elizabeth gagged, and he pulled again, ramming himself past her resistance and deep into her.

"Bitch."

He speared into her again and again.

It was almost too much. He almost lost control. That would never do.

He jerked back away from her. Elizabeth was probably too far gone into shock to realize now what was being done to her.

He flung her down, her head cracking hard and hollow against the pack dirt of the basement floor, and he fell on top of her, forcing her knees apart and slamming himself into her body.

There was that moment of lovely, sweet resistance and then the sensation of flesh tearing as he pushed past the virgin-whore obstruction, and he was fully inside. Filling her. Saving her. Giving her so much more than he received.

He hunched his back and drove again and again inside her, the path lubricated now by blood.

Dane laughed with the purest joy and battered her flesh with his. He stuffed the fingers of his left hand deep into her mouth, filling her there at the same time as he filled her cunt. With his right hand he fumbled in his pocket for the tiny knife he had prepared so carefully.

He was close now. His excitement was rising past the point of any control.

As the critical moment came, as the pressures built and built and reached explosive force inside him, the shiny tip of the little blade found its nest beneath whore-Elizabeth's left ear.

In spite of everything, she must have felt and recognized the prick of the steel. She tried to twist away, but his hand clamped inside her mouth with an iron strength and he held her immobile.

A push. Not difficult. Almost gentle. And the hot blood of her body flowed over his hand and bathed his wrist.

Donnie—Dane—roared out the laughter of his joy, and the great, cleansing explosion of his release flooded out of his loins and into hers. Draining him. Releasing her from all evil. Anointing the Jezebel with the purifying fluids.

"Oh, God," Dane whispered. "Dear God." He shuddered and felt his passion ease. Felt himself fall limp although still inside Elizabeth's body.

Silently those huge, pale eyes stared at him, still aware, still perceiving while the life force pumped out of her and into the dirt of the floor.

She was already too weak to resist any more now.

Dane withdrew his hand from her mouth and bent his head to kiss her with a warm and gentle love.

Elizabeth was safe now from all sin and tribulation.

In a way, he envied her the peace and forgiveness that now were hers.

He kissed her again, slow and lingering and ineffably gentle.

"I love you," he said with a tender smile.

CHAPTER ELEVEN

There was no trick to finding the small village where Douglas Fogarty had been captured. The job was time-consuming but not difficult. They hired a buggy and drove out the road where the wagon had been found with the bodies of the sheriff and driver and simply started asking questions. Anyone could have done the same, including the dead sheriff's deputies. That they hadn't was a reflection of their belief that the murderer had already escaped over the border into Canada and could likely be written off as lost.

Actually, Raider was not sure that they were wrong. But unlike them, he would push it. And cross the border after Fogarty/Fallon if necessary. Allan never had exactly told him not to.

"Sure, I remember the guy," the innkeeper in a town called Yelm told them. "Hadn't planned to stop here, I guess, but the stage busted an axle and had to lay over. The young fella—I think he said his name was Fargo—he paid in advance for his lodging an' went out looking for dinner. Never come back that I know of. Left his things an' all. Just never come back."

"Did you report him missing?" Manton asked.

The innkeeper looked at him and shrugged. "Wasn't none of my business what the fella wanted to do. Besides, we got no law in town. Didn't see no point in making a fuss outa something that wasn't my affair."

All of which meant, Raider figured, that the innkeeper would cheerfully hold on to the abandoned luggage for a while and then claim it for storage fees. Raider was willing to bet there would be no cash left in the luggage by now, regardless of whether there had been to begin with.

Raider flashed his credentials, not giving the innkeeper time enough to examine them closely. The fellow was welcome to assume anything he wanted about Raider's status with the law.

"I want to inspect that luggage," Raider said. "And while I'm doing that I want you to check back in your register to see what name he was using here."

"I expect you c'n look at the bags if you're of a mind to, but I don't keep no register, Officer."

Raider grunted and let the man lead them into a storage shed tacked on to the back of the two-story log building.

He could feel Ted Manton's excitement when the innkeeper pointed to the pair of handsomely crafted leather bags that were gathering dust in a corner of the shed.

Both of them were of the best and most expensive quality. More important, both of them carried small brass plaques set into the lockplates with the initials D.F. engraved in the metal.

This was definitely Fogarty/Fallon/Shitface's luggage.

Manton tried to open the spring locks. They didn't budge.

Raider knelt beside the larger bag and took out his knife.

"Officer, I don't know as you oughta . . ."

Raider ignored him. He wedged the knife blade into the flimsy lock and applied pressure. The lock snapped open easily. Most locks, he realized, are for honest people. They will stop a casual snoop but hardly slow anyone with criminal intent.

"Officer . . ." the innkeeper tried again.

Raider was amused by the protest. The dinky little locks must actually have stopped the man from opening the bags. He probably was having visions of any cash stored in there flying out of his grasp with Raider's appearance.

Raider shoved the open bag toward Manton and jim-
mied the lock on the second case.

The results were disappointing.

An address book would have been wonderful. Any clue
would have been welcome. What they found in Fogarty/
Fallon's luggage was clothing, lotions and ointments, hair-
brushes, a much used small whetstone, a New Testament
with the unhelpful inscription "To D.F. from G.F." and a
few other items of little interest.

"Damn," Raider said.

"Yeah," Manton agreed.

"Officer . . ."

"Shut up," Raider told the man wearily.

There were no letters, no pictures, absolutely nothing of
a personal nature that might help them.

The clothing, Raider noticed, even the underthings,
were all of the highest quality. Everything was clean.
Everything was neatly folded and tidy.

"It isn't much to go on," Manton said.

Raider shrugged. "It tells us a little. It tells us he didn't
act on the spur of the moment. That killing wasn't on any
whim."

Manton raised an eyebrow.

Raider pointed to the open bags. "Take a look at the
clothes in there. What d'you see?"

Ted Manton shrugged. "Very nice clothing. Custom-tai-
lored shirts. Silk smallclothes. Nothing really interesting."

Raider grinned. "Take another look. It's all clean. No
dirty laundry in there, is there?"

"I . . . suppose not. Now that you mention it."

"He's a fussy son of a bitch, our D.F.," Raider said.
"Very neat. Very well organized. No dirty socks in his luggage. No soiled underwear. Not a limp collar in the lot.
Think about that. The bastard planned everything right to
the last detail an' even had his laundry done up fresh before he was ready to murder that girl an' skip ahead of the
law. The man here says he stopped in Yelm 'cause of a
broken stage axle. He hadn't planned that. If the axle

hadn't broke, he'd've been long away and Sheriff Simmons never would've caught him and never would've died. So we've learned a little more about him, Ted. Not much, true, an' for sure not what we wanted. But it's another little piece of information we can add to what we know."

"Clever," Manton said.

"Not really." Raider smiled at him. "But there's times when persistent is better'n clever. With this SOB I think it's persistence we need right now."

Manton nodded. Raider stood, ignoring the bags that stood open on the floor. "Your customer won't be coming back after these," he told the innkeeper. "You can do what you want with them."

The man looked like he didn't know whether he should be pleased that the things were his now or disappointed that there was nothing of value for him to appropriate.

"Where do we go now, Raider?"

"Back to Olympia. See if Allan's come to an understanding with Western Union yet."

They headed back out to the hired buggy.

CHAPTER TWELVE

As soon as they walked in the door of the Western Union office, Raider knew that a response had been received there. Although he wasn't sure which way it was going.

"You smart-ass son of a bitch," Hargreve snarled.

Raider smiled at him.

"I don't think—"

"Good," Raider said. "Keep it that way." Ignoring the manager for the moment, he went to the counter and asked if there was a wire for him.

The clerk on duty gave his boss an unhappy glance but sorted through the pigeonholes in his desk for the appropriate slip and handed it over. The message was from Allan himself. It read:

COMPLIANCE ASSURED STOP CITE GENERAL MANAGER BRASFORD IF NECESSARY STOP GOOD LUCK STOP

The Scot's usual brevity, based on telegraph fees being assessed on a per-word basis, was apparent in the early part of the message form. But that addition of the unnecessary "good luck" part was an indication of Allan Pinkerton's personal belief in the importance of this one. Raider was impressed.

"I take it you got a message too," Raider said to Hargreve.

The man mumbled something that Raider did not hear —which was probably just as well—and gestured sharply to his clerk, then turned and walked away into the privacy of his office, slamming the door behind him. Raider

chuckled and winked at Ted Manton, who was still standing in some confusion behind him.

"Good news?" Manton asked.

"Uh huh." Raider handed him the message form and
looked expectantly at the Western Union clerk.

The clerk pulled a thick loose-leaf file out and gave it to
Raider. It was the ledger containing records of every bank
draft transaction conducted in this Western Union district
for the current year. The man handed it across without any
display of the emotion his employer would have shown. It
was no skin off his nose what happened here, so long as he
was doing what he was told by the people who paid him.

"Thanks."

Raider carried the file down to the end of the counter,
sorry there were no desks provided for customer use but
damn sure not inclined to ask for the additional favor of a
place to sit. With Manton at his elbow, he began going
through the records.

"D. F. Osgood," Manton said. "That's my guess. I have
a feeling about that one."

Raider shrugged. Hunches were wonderful. Sometimes.
But he had learned a long time back to trust them only so
far. There were four likely names to choose from in the
approximate time frame. The killer could be any one of
them. Or none. The bastard might have settled on the initials D.F. for no reason other than a whim. At this point it
was just too early to tell.

"It could be," he admitted, "but we'll try and cross-ref-
erence *every* name, not just that one."

Manton nodded and began writing down a list of every
name of every draft customer appearing in the file for a
period of four weeks prior to Beth Armister's murder.
Every name, not just the ones showing the initials D. F.
Raider insisted on it.

At the head of the list, though, were four names in particular, which Manton wrote down, with D. F. Osgood at the top.

The four primary suspects were Osgood, D. George Franklin, Dane Florette, and Donald H. Fisch.

In all there were thirty-seven possible suspects on the list.

Any of them, Raider realized, could be their man under his true name.

The only draft customers Raider did not insist should be included were corporate accounts maintained with Western Union, and the only reason he let those go by was that the amounts involved in those transfers were unreasonably large for a single person on the road, no matter how big a spender the SOB might be when he wasn't murdering young girls.

"What now?" Manton asked when the list was completed and a copy of it was in each man's coat pocket.

Raider thought for a moment, then pursed his lips. "San Francisco, I think."

"Why in the hell would we want to go to San Francisco now?"

"We want to cross-check this list. Fallon—or Osgood or Franklin or whoever the hell he might be—killed in Kansas City and San Francisco that we're sure of. He would've sent a wire again from someplace within prob'ly two hundred miles of here after he escaped from Sheriff Simmons. But we don't know where that wire would've gone out from. He might've gone to Canada like the police suspect. Or he might not've. It could take us weeks to chase down the telegraph office he used after he left this area. Months, maybe. So we aren't gonna waste that amount of time. We go either to Kansas City or to San Francisco. And San Francisco's closer."

"Seattle . . ." Manton ventured.

"Seattle is a guess," Raider insisted. "He could as easily have gone south or east from here. San Francisco is the surest bet. That's where we get another list. Say, from the date that girl there was murdered and before it a month,

month and a half. We go through those records and look for any one of the names on this list." He tapped his coat pocket, causing the paper there to rattle softly. "Anybody shows on the Olympia file *and* the San Francisco records, he's likely our boy."

"Then what?"

Raider pretended not to have heard the question as he turned and headed for the hotel to begin packing. The truth was, he wasn't sure yet.

One step at a time, he told himself. One step at a damned time.

CHAPTER THIRTEEN

Dwayne Forbes stepped off the Southern Pacific passenger coach and relinquished his bag to a porter.

He could not remember ever having felt so good, so alive before.

The afternoon sunshine felt warm on his face, and the air here was so clear and gentle he could scarcely believe it.

Off to the east he could see a jagged line of low mountains. Somewhere out of view to the west would be the ocean. Excursions to the beach, he thought with contentment, would be a marvelous diversion in the weeks to come.

Best of all, though, was the deep satisfaction and inner peace that came from knowing what he had done for Elizabeth.

She had been such a lovely thing. And now she was safe for all time. Knowing that gave him a sense of warmth that made it all worthwhile. Everything.

"Rig, suh?"

Dane's head snapped around as he was startled out of his reverie. "What?"

"I asked would you like a rig, suh? Or are you bein' met?"

"Oh." Dwayne gave the helpful porter a happy, boyish smile. "I'll need a cab."

"Very good, suh." The porter hurried ahead, lifting one hand to his mouth to execute a piercingly shrill whistle, and immediately a small, closed buggy was brought up, its high-stepping sorrel coming to a snappy halt and the driver jumping down to load Dwayne's bag into the luggage boot and help his passenger inside with a flourish.

"Where to, sir?"

"I'll be staying for some time, possibly several months," Dwayne said. After that incredibly delightful experience with Elizabeth he was beginning to realize that he was not taking time enough to savor his experiences and to anticipate them properly. Speed was important, of course. There was only so much a person could expect to accomplish in one lifetime. But surely he was entitled to some relaxation and enjoyment for himself as well. Surely God would permit him that small luxury. "I shall want the very finest accommodations possible," he told the driver. "Something, I think, with a view. And close to the better churches." He smiled.

"The Sherson-by-the-Sea is our finest, sir. But quite expensive."

Dwayne's smile did not alter. "The Sherson-by-the-Sea would be just fine then, my good fellow."

"Yes, sir." The driver smiled, instantly falling under the handsome young gentleman's charm. "My pleasure, sir."

With a touch of his hatbrim he settled the gentleman onto the mohair upholstery of the cab and made sure the door was securely latched. Then, with a completely unnecessary but rather fancy crack of his whip, the man put the sorrel into a swift trot.

This was a fine, fine day, Dwayne reflected with pleasure as he enjoyed the scenery along the way.

Wonderful things were going to happen to him here. He was sure of it.

CHAPTER FOURTEEN

"Shit!"

"Something wrong?"

"Yes, damn it, there is something wrong," Raider said with frustration. "There's *two* names that match here."

"May I see?" The San Francisco office manager for Western Union pulled the register around to face him and adjusted his reading glasses.

At least this fellow was being helpful. Unlike Hargreve in Olympia, the man in charge of the divisional office here was willing to do anything he could to assist Raider and Manton once he checked with the home office for permission.

"Oh, yes," he said, referring back several times to the Olympia list in Manton's firm handwriting. "So I see. Mr. D. F. Osgood and a, um, Dane Florette. Both appear on our register."

Raider nodded glumly. This development was not something he had foreseen.

Still, damn it, it brought the suspects down to just two. That was a damn sight better than thirty-seven, any way you wanted to slice it.

"I may be able to help," the Western Union manager said.

"How's that?"

"I believe Mr. Manton mentioned that you are looking for a young man who has committed, um, several heinous murders?"

"That's right."

"As it happens, sir, I am aquainted with Mr. Osgood."

"Yes?"

The Western Union man smiled. "Douglas Fir Osgood is what everyone calls him, although not generally in his hearing. Actually I don't know his true names. Douglas Fir certainly fits, though. Mr. Osgood is a lease broker for timber operations. You know. Lumber. Industrial timbers. Wood pulp for the manufacture of paper products. Like that."

"Yes?" Manton was becoming excited now. Hell, so was Raider.

"Mr. Osgood is a gentleman in his early sixties, I should say. He does quite a lot of business through our office."

"Hot damn!" Raider said with a snap of his fingers. "That means Dane Florette is our man."

"I should expect so," the Western Union man said.

"Do you know anything about Florette?"

The manager shook his head. "I've no knowledge about him, I'm afraid. Let me check our files, though. The only information we have on the register here is the name. We might have a copy of the transaction elsewhere. If you will excuse me?"

Raider was damn sure willing to let the man do anything he wanted as long as there was the slimmest chance that it might help.

The Western Union manager disappeared toward the back of the office, and Raider and Manton began to pace the lobby impatiently.

"Dane Florette," Manton repeated quietly several times. "Dane Florette. My God, Raider, do you realize that after all this time I finally know who it was who murdered my darling Liz. Dane Florette." The pale father was trembling.

"Don't get your hopes too high," Raider cautioned.

The caution was wasted, of course. Manton's hopes were extremely high. And so were Raider's.

This was the first solid lead anyone had realized, and it had taken the Pinkerton Agency the third attempt to get just this far.

But it was a lead, damn it. And it was solid. It was a base they could build on.

Persistence, Raider had told Manton. It was dogged persistence that would eventually break the killer.

And now they knew who the killer really was.

The cover of false names had been stripped away.

Now Raider had to find a way to make the rest of it follow.

He was still excited when the Western Union manager returned holding a dusty and somewhat dog-earred file folder.

"I have our copies of the transactions for that period, Mr. Raider," he said.

"And Florette's?"

The man smiled and nodded. He pulled out a pair of sheets pinned together and laid them on the counter facing Raider and Manton.

"This is perfect," Raider said.

"I hope it will help."

The sheets were both messages bearing Dane Florette's name, the two forms dated four days apart.

The first was Florette's request for funds. The second was the response.

The first was addressed to a D. C. Florette, 24 Cable Street, Hartford, Connecticut. It was terse almost to the point of being rude, stating simply that the sender was in need of funds and requesting an immediate draft for $5,000.

The second sheet was the Western Union office copy of a bank draft authorization for $3,000, payable to Dane C. Florette III. That sheet was receipted for in Florette's own hand, the ink faded slightly but still perfectly clear.

"There wasn't any message sent with the money?" Raider asked.

The Western Union man shook his head. "Apparently not. I'm sure a copy would have been attached had there been one. Just the draft authorization, as you see here."

Manton bent close over the document. Raider could see

that the man was in a state of agitation when he stared down at the very handwriting of the man who had so brutally murdered his daughter.

"Funny that there wouldn't have been a message," Raider said aloud.

"Yes, but I'm sure there was none. I am very particular with my staff about records-keeping. If there had been a message, it should have been included. I feel sure it would have been."

That was interesting, Raider realized. And possibly revealing. Florette asked for $5,000. He received $3,000. His note to Daddy had been abrupt. There was no note at all in return. Just the money.

Raider copied down the father's Connecticut address and the dates of the wires. The bank draft had been received by Florette eight days before Betty Crane was murdered here in San Francisco.

It fit, damn it. It all fit.

Raider bent close to the again grieving Manton, and he too closely examined the signature of the man they sought.

Florette's handwriting was bold and sure. No hasty scrawl here but a proud, firm wielding of the pen. The script was classically styled, with the characteristic loops and sworls of a well-educated person who in childhood had been carefully drilled in proper penmanship.

That only made sense, of course. A young man whose father could wire him funds in the thousands would certainly have received a good education.

What the bastard had chosen to do with his knowledge was something else, of course.

Raider thanked the Western Union manager profusely, and Manton wrung the man's hand in teary-eyed gratitude.

"Let's go, Ted."

"Where?"

"You aren't gonna like this."

Manton raised an eyebrow.

"I think our next stop's in Connecticut."

"Florette is still here in the West," Manton protested. "I'm sure of that, Raider. I can feel it."

Raider did not bother to mention the feeling Manton had had a few days earlier about lumberman D. F. Osgood being their man. The truth was that this time he happened to agree with Ted Manton. He too believed that Dane Florette was somewhere in the West. But to find the son of a bitch, they needed information from D. C. Florette in Connecticut.

And you just don't go asking a man about his son the murderer by way of an impersonal telegraph message.

For this they would have to be face to face with the man.

CHAPTER FIFTEEN

Manton paid off the cabby, and Raider hauled both their bags out of the hack. There was an eastbound passenger train due to leave the old Central Pacific depot in forty-five minutes, which gave them plenty of time, although Ted Manton was of the fussbudget sort who always likes to be early rather than risk being late for anything.

They passed through the wrought-iron gatework onto the platform, and Manton paused to buy a newspaper from a freckled kid nearby.

Raider walked on, admiring a nicely dressed young woman already waiting on the platform. She was seated on a bench with her legs crossed, and there was a most interesting display of shapely ankle on view. The man she was with was considerably older than she, with steely gray showing at his temples. He was one lucky SOB, Raider thought. Unless of course he was her father. In that case the poor guy probably had plenty to worry about. She was a real beauty, with auburn hair and—

"Oh, Jesus!!"

Raider turned.

Ted Manton had been trailing a few paces behind, glancing at the headlines in the local paper while he walked.

Now he had come to an abrupt halt and was white-faced and trembling. Even from a distance of some yards Raider could see the way his tremors were making the newspaper shake. Raider hurried back to him.

"What's wrong?"

Manton squeezed his eyes shut and shook his head. Blindly he shoved the paper out for Raider to see: "Debutante Slain: Academy Pupil Foully Murdered in Church Basement." The gray column of newsprint beneath the startling headline was long.

Raider tucked the newspaper into his pocket and took Manton by the elbow. He had to half support the man to the nearest bench and help him to a seat before he could even think about reading the article. Manton looked like a man who has just been sucker-punched in the windpipe.

"Porter! Bring the gentleman a glass of water, please. Quickly."

The porter needed no explanations. One look at Manton was enough to convince anyone that he was sick. The porter hurried away, and Raider grabbed for the newspaper again.

"A young lady of quality of this community was yesterday found cruelly murdered in the basement of the First Episcopal Church, Henley and Broad Streets. The child, enrolled as a pupil of Miss Barkley's academy for young women, was identified as Miss Elizabeth O'Neill, aged 16, daughter of Mr. and Mrs. Anthony O'Neill, California Street. Her body was discovered in the forenoon by the Rev. O. B. Wirth, pastor of the church where the disagreeable incident occurred. A search had been under way for the missing girl since the previous evening, when she failed to return home from visiting friends. Police Chief Justin Carling and said Miss O'Neill died of stab wounds. She had been . . ."

The article ran on at some length. Apparently some local editor with a good memory had added to it here, because a comparison was drawn between the deaths of the O'Neill girl and the much earlier murder in San Francisco of Miss Elizabeth (Betty) Crane under seemingly similar circumstances.

The original report submitted by wire from a correspondent was datelined Fresno, California.

"Damn," Raider groaned aloud.

The porter returned with a cup of water and a flask of brandy as well. The man had Manton drink from both, then withdrew before Raider thought to offer him a tip for his helpfulness.

"I . . . Sorry, Raider. I wasn't prepared for that."

"I understand, Ted. It got to me, too."

"Yes, I can see that it has." Manton looked better. He took a deep breath and stood. He was shaky on his feet but seemed to be recovering.

"We won't be going east just yet, Ted. I won't, anyway. This, uh, might be pretty rough for you. Maybe it'd be better if you waited here while I go down to Fresno and see if there's anything I can learn."

Manton shook his head, and his face twisted in mingled anger and anguish. "No, Raider. I have to be there. I have to."

"If you think you're up to it."

"I am up to whatever is required," Manton said quietly but with force.

Raider nodded and hurried off to find out about transportation to Fresno.

When he returned he looked thoughtful.

"What's—"

Raider shushed Manton with a gesture and once again bent to read the newspaper article, this time more closely. "There's something . . ." He shook his head. "Never mind. It'll come to me."

Later, on the train, Raider snapped his fingers and turned to Manton, who was fitfully trying to doze on the hard seat of the jolting passenger coach.

"Your daughter, Ted."

"Yes?"

"You call her Liz or Lizzie."

"That's right. My little Lizzie."

"Is Liz her full name, Ted?"

"No. A pet name only." He tried a smile, but the expression wouldn't come. He only managed to look wistful and sad instead.

"What was her actual name, Ted?"

"What? Oh. I . . . I was elsewhere, I'm afraid. You want to know my Liz's name? Why, it was Elizabeth, of course."

"I'll be damned," Raider said.

"I don't understand."

"Look, I don't know if it means anything at all, Ted, but something just struck me. After that newspaper article, I mean. The girl who was murdered in San Francisco. Her name was Betty, right?"

Manton nodded.

"Right. But the guy who put this story together wrote it down as Elizabeth, an' then he put the name Betty inside those curvy things . . . what d'they call 'em . . . ?"

"Parentheses."

"Yeah, them. Anyhow, he put her name down as really being Elizabeth and Betty a nickname. And the girl in Olympia, she was called Beth. But Beth is a pretty common shortening of Elizabeth. And now I find out your little girl was named Elizabeth though she was called Liz. Like I say, Ted, I don't know what it means or how it'll help. But all those girls being named Elizabeth, that's just too damn much for coincidence. You know?"

"But what possible connection could there be in a name?"

"I've no idea, Ted. But I don't much believe in coincidence to begin with. And *all* the victims with the same name? No way I can think that's by accident. It means something, Ted. I just wish to God I knew what."

"We'll ask his father?" Manton suggested hesitantly.

"You bet we will. Unless we find something in Fresno that points the finger to where Dane Florette III has gone next."

Manton shuddered and peered out the window at the passing countryside. The trip and the strain of the hunt for his daughter's killer were wearing on him. He was drawn and looked even unhealthier than when Raider had met him back in Chicago.

But then, it was no damned picnic for Raider, either, and he wasn't emotionally involved in the manhunt. At least he wasn't supposed to be. But with this prick Florette, the more Raider learned about him, the more Raider wanted him.

The train rattled on toward Fresno.

CHAPTER SIXTEEN

Chief of Police Justin Carling was a big man on the downhill side of middle age. His hair used to be red, but now his Burnside whiskers were nearly white, and he had a considerable gut on him. His suit was handsomely tailored, and he affected flashy rings and stickpins. At first meeting Raider decided the man was probably more politician than lawman.

Carling stuck his hand out and invited them inside, though, without wasting any time about it.

"My sergeant tells me you're here to ask about the O'Neill murder."

"That's right." Raider introduced himself and Manton.

Carling nodded and motioned them toward a pair of chairs in front of his desk. "You didn't come here like those damn bloodsucking spectators that're gawking at the front of the church, so why don't you tell me what does bring you to Fresno."

Raider was beginning to suspect that his first impression of Chief Carling may have been far short of the mark. Manton kept quiet about his own sorrows while Raider filled the chief in.

"You say you might have an idea of who killed that girl?" Carling asked at one point.

Raider nodded.

"I have my own ideas, of course," Carling said. "No proof, unfortunately. There weren't any witnesses that we've located yet, although I have men going door to door in the residential sections between where the girl was last seen on Thursday evening and the church building where she was found Friday. I notice you haven't asked me exactly how she died or, uh, about certain other details."

"If we're right in our suspicions, chief, we can tell you without asking," Raider told him.

"You go right ahead then, young fella, and see if you can tell me what wasn't in the newspaper yet. An' won't be if I have my say about it."

"If the murder was committed by our suspect," Raider said, "the girl will have been sexually assaulted. That wasn't in the papers, I noticed. And she will have died by a single knife thrust under her left ear. Right about here." Raider reached up and touched the side of his own neck to point to the spot Dane Florette favored in his murders.

Carling snapped upright in his chair and leaned forward. "I'll be damned."

"If you have a suspect in mind, as I gather you do, we would also guess that the man's initials are D.F. Whatever name he was using here isn't his own, of course."

"Don Flynn," Carling said. "He was a new member of a church youth group the girl attended. The only reason we suspect him is because he checked out of his hotel the next morning. Said something about going to Virginia City over in Nevada to see the Comstock and that he'd be back later. But he didn't leave any luggage stored at the hotel and made no return reservations. I've wired the authorities there to watch for him and hold him for questioning if he shows."

"He won't," Raider said flatly. "If that's where he said he was going, that's the last place he'd really go. Wherever he went from here, he'll be using a different name now."

"And you think you know who he is?"

"Dane Florette," Raider said. "His family home is in Connecticut. Apparently he hasn't been back there in some time. He gets his funds by Western Union draft and travels a lot. So far he's killed in Kansas City, San Francisco, Olympia, and now here. That we know of. There could be others, probably are, in fact, that we aren't aware of. For some reason all the girls are named Elizabeth."

"Son of a bitch," Carling said. "Excuse me a minute." He left the office and was back shortly afterward. "I don't know if it will do any good," he said, "but I told my sergeant to get a wire off warning the law to look out for anybody by this Florette's description and using the initials D.F. Pity the bastard's gone from here. I'd like to have him in my jail."

"Chief, I'd like to see him in anybody's jail."

"I'll settle for that."

"Is there . . . is there anything we can do to help?" Manton asked. "The family, I mean. I know how difficult this period can be."

Carling shook his head. "Damned nice of you to offer, mister, but there isn't anything will make this easier on them. Solid people, though. They'll work it through. The preacher is over there again today, I understand. The burial was yesterday. The whole town's pretty well shaken by it. My wife took a cake to them and some other things. Not that anybody's interested in all that food at times like this, but it's good to remind folks that their neighbors care. That's what it's all about, you know. Showing that you care and want to help."

No, Raider decided, Carling wasn't just a politician drawing pay from the public.

"Tell me one thing if you can," Carling asked, leaning forward again.

"If we can."

"Why? That's the thing that's been graveling me ever since that child's body was found. Why would he want to hurt her like that? It wasn't just to get his rocks off. The way I understand it, he had money and is a good-looking kid. Plenty of opportunity for pussy if that's what he wanted, so I got to conclude that that wasn't what he was after. Yet he raped that girl and then murdered her."

"It doesn't make any sense, Chief. Not any more than the fact that all his victims are named Elizabeth."

"There has to be a reason," Carling said. "There's a

reason for every damn thing. Crazy reason sometimes, but there's always a reason."

"When we figure out Florette's reason," Raider said, "we'll be that much closer to catching him."

"I wonder if it would do any good to ask his family," Carling mused.

"We intend to do exactly that, Chief. We came here hoping to learn something new, but our next step is in Connecticut."

Carling rubbed his chin. "I was thinking of sending a telegram."

"Please don't do that, Chief. A question like that coming at them out of the blue . . . I mean, surely they can't know what the kid is like. There's no telling how they might react. I want to be there and talk to them eye to eye."

The police chief thought about that for a moment, then nodded. "Makes sense. If I had the budget for it, I'd send an officer with you." His expression hardened. "One thing, Detective."

"Yes?"

"When you run this bastard to ground, assuming you get him before I can—not so unlikely considering how limited my jurisdiction is—he's got to be tried somewhere. I'd sure like it to be here."

"I don't know—" Manton began.

Carling cut him off. "Let me tell you why. And if it ever leaves this room, I'll call you both liars. I know how to play dirty when I have to. If this Dane Florette or Don Flynn or whoever the hell he is winds up being tried in my town, gentlemen, I can absolutely guarantee you that he'll end his life swinging from a rope. All legal and proper and no time for appeals. You hear what I'm saying?"

Raider only nodded, but Ted Manton reached forward and solemnly shook the police chief's hand on it.

"That's a guarantee I wouldn't be able to get back home," Manton said.

"Well, it's one you can have here. You boys bring this

Florette to me, and he won't be murdering any more innocent girls. Or anybody else either. I can promise you that
much."

"You'd have to build a good case against him," Raider
said.

"You find him; I'll have the legal case built. I told you
my boys are already scouring the neighborhood for anybody who might've seen them together that night. Time
you put irons on Florette, I'll have my witnesses. Comes to
that, I can always scare up a surprise eyewitness. Like
maybe a drunk who saw the whole thing but didn't come
forward to testify till he sobered up." Carling paused re-
flectively. "A feeling just come over me, boys. I think
maybe there *was* a drunk who saw the whole thing. And if
I had to guess, I'd say that he'll sober up and come talk to
me sometime in the next day or two." The chief gave them
a slow smile. "What do you think about my hunch, boys?
Care to make a wager on it?"

"I was always taught that you don't bet into a pat hand,"
Raider said.

"Is there anything else I can do for you?"

Raider shook his head, but Manton spoke up.

"There is one thing, Chief. I'd like you to deputize me
or appoint me a special police officer on your force. Whatever you call it."

"No reason why I couldn't do that, Mr. Manton," Carling said.

Raider gave the client a questioning look, but Manton
was paying attention only to the chief at the moment. Deliberately, Raider suspected.

It was a damned odd request, Raider thought, but Manton tucked Justin Carling's tin badge into his pocket and
refused to talk about if afterward.

CHAPTER SEVENTEEN

For one agonizing moment *he could not remember his own name*. Then, his smile steadying, he extended his hand. "Dwayne Forbes," he said.

The young man introduced himself, shook hands, and chatted idly for a few minutes before drifting away to the punch bowl and a conversation with a group of other young men, all of whom seemed to be involved with a local shooting club for young gentlemen of quality.

Dwayne relaxed to such an extent that he uncharacteristically leaned against a wall.

The moment of forgetfulness was past, but it had frightened him. Nothing like that had ever happened to him before. For that terrible moment, Florette was the only name that he could remember. And Florette was *not* his name. The name Florette belonged to someone else entirely. Dwayne might use it now and again when he had to. When he had to deal, for instance, with that old bastard back east. But the name Florette no longer really belonged to him. Nor would he want to claim it if he could.

He knew what the problem was, of course, the problem that had led to his momentary confusion.

He had been thinking about Elizabeth. About all of them. Damn them.

Damn that old man and damn the Jezebel most of all.

Damn them for . . .

He shook himself, the physical gesture forcing the return of his thoughts to here and now.

He'd been doing it again, damn it.

93

The past presence of Dane Florette once again had been interfering with the hopes and the dreams of Dwayne Forbes.

Across the room, Pastor Kiner smiled at Dwayne. Dwayne grinned at the preacher and extended to Kiner a silent toast with the raising of his cup.

Pastor Kiner was a revelation to Dwayne. A positive revelation and a hint of great promise for the future.

Because Pastor Kiner was a very young man. Only twenty-six. Dane Florette was twenty-five. Dwayne Forbes could be too if he wanted.

Somehow it had never occurred to Dwayne before that anyone so young could have charge of his very own flock.

The possibilities of that were . . . limitless.

Dwayne might one day choose to have *his* very own flock of devoted parishioners.

He would be successful at it. He knew in his heart that he could be. Would be if he so chose.

It was a marvelous thought. Presenting much more opportunity than anything he had ever conceived before now.

It would require little more than determination. Dwayne had that. Firm determination and a bit of luck.

Why, from a position like that, with a pulpit of his own, there was nothing he could not accomplish.

Dwayne smiled again.

Not here, though. At least not in this particular church.

Here there was no Delilah who needed his help to return to grace.

That was unfortunate, really.

Oh, there were girls in the group who were pretty enough. Mayva, for instance. She was really very pretty. And a trifle flirtatious. Dwayne had been able to see that practically from the first moment he saw her.

But Mayva was not the whore. It was Elizabeth who was the whore. It was Elizabeth who needed his help, and there was no Elizabeth here. Only Mayva who was pretty and a flirt but was not the great whore in need of salvation.

That was a shame, really. Dwayne would have enjoyed

these young people. He liked them. He would have been pleased with an opportunity to spend time with them. Instead he would have to look elsewhere. What he had to do was much too important for him to spend time with this group who did not have Elizabeth to threaten and defile them.

Dwayne sighed. Still, even if he was not needed in this place at this moment, it was a revelation to him that he could—should—have a flock of his own. So this visit had been no waste. It was, in fact, a great step forward.

His smile returned, and he crossed the room to place his empty cup on the table beside the punch bowl.

"I say, Forbes," one of the young gentlemen greeted him. "You wouldn't be a marksman by any chance?"

Dwayne shook his head. "Neither by chance nor design, I'm afraid. I know nothing about firearms."

"That's a pity, Forbes. We're in need of another member on our team. Can't fairly compete for the all-around trophy with a short-handed squad, you know."

"I wish I could help," Dwayne said in perfect honesty. He truly enjoyed being able to help his brothers and sisters.

"Would you consider taking up the sport?" another boy asked. "It isn't so hard to learn."

"Oh, I've never been one for athletics," Dwayne said.

"But this is different. No strenuous activity involved in shooting, Forbes. Very pleasant, actually. And of course there's no injury done to any living thing. Just poking holes in bits of paper, you see."

Dwayne smiled. It wasn't blood that bothered him, although he could understand someone mistakenly thinking so. Quite to the contrary, Dwayne knew better than most that blood is the force of life and the symbol of salvation. And the purest instrument of baptism.

"We really could use another member," a third boy said. "We're all involved, you know. Our problem is that there are just too few of us."

"Henry could teach you," the second boy suggested. "Henry's the best shot in the county. The rest of us feel badly that we drag him down. With another club he would be champion for sure." Henry was the boy Dwayne had just met.

The young men, five of them, crowded closer around Dwayne to try and cajole him into joining their group.

"You'd be a whiz at it," someone said. "A steady hand and a clear eye is all that's required. We can see at a glance you have that."

"And I've a rifle you could use," another said. "Not quite the finest quality but good enough."

"Good enough if someone else is using it," another boy teased, slapping his friend on the shoulder.

One of them laughed. "Unfortunately for Tom, an expensive rifle isn't difference enough at the target butts. It needs that clear eye and steady hand. Which is it you lack, Tom? The clear eye or the steady hand?"

The boy named Tom grunted. "It's the breathing that does me in. I see Mayva watching, and my breathing goes all to pieces."

The rest of them, including Dwayne, laughed at the admission.

"Do say you'll join us, Forbes," one of them pleaded.

"We'll teach you all you know and loan you the equipment. You'd enjoy it. Truly you would," said another.

"Let me think about it," Dwayne said gently. "If I change my mind, I shall certainly let you all know."

"We'd be ever so grateful if you would."

"I'll think about it."

The truth, of course, was that he had no intention of remaining with this group. They were the first he had visited here. He truly liked them. They were an enjoyable group.

But Dwayne was not needed here.

The whore Elizabeth was not among them.

The need for him lay somewhere else. In some other youth group. He only hoped that that need could be met here in this city. He liked it here. The town, the ocean, all the friendly people. It was a grand place, and he was enjoying the time he was able to spend here.

"You'll think about it, then?"

"Yes, I'll think about it," Dwayne promised.

It was late enough that the first few members of the group had begun to disperse toward their homes. Dwayne Forbes said goodbye to the other boys and crossed the room to express his thanks to Pastor Kiner. He had no intention of returning to this group, of course, but it would have been churlish to neglect proper etiquette.

He went out into the delightful cool of the evening and enjoyed the tang of sea salt on the air as he walked back toward the hotel.

CHAPTER EIGHTEEN

The trip east had been long and tiring if not really difficult, and by the time they arrived Raider thought Ted Manton looked more like he should be in a hospital ward than in the seat of a cab.

The man hadn't been the picture of health to begin with. Now his skin had a gray, ashen color to it, and the bags under his eyes were big enough to pack a week's clothing into. He looked, Raider thought, like a skull with some half-tanned skin draped over it.

"It's early enough," Manton said. "I still think we should tell the driver to take us to Florette's address, and—"

"Damn it, Ted, if you ain't about to drop, I am." It wasn't all that much of a lie. The days of train travel had been tiring enough for anyone. "Besides, it's too late in the afternoon to start in on the man. This is gonna be bad enough without us jumping him when he's late for dinner or pissed off from the day's business. We'll wait until he's fresh an' rested an' nothing's gone wrong in the day. Till we show up, that is. We'll wait until morning."

Manton protested, but Raider noticed that when he finally did give in and settle back in his seat his eyes dragged shut almost on their own, and his breathing slowed in restless sleep.

The way Manton looked right now, Raider wasn't willing to bet that he would have a live client by the time this case was done. Yet the fellow wouldn't consider slowing down, much less quitting. Raider had spent half the trip trying to convince Manton to leave the train and go home to Kansas City while he finished the job for him.

The hotel the cab brought them to was older than most you might find on the good side of the Mississippi but no better that Raider could see. It just had more soot built up to blacken the mortar between the bricks.

They checked into a shared room. Raider didn't bother to unpack, and neither did Manton. Raider's reason was that he didn't figure to be here long enough for it to be worthwhile. Manton's was that as soon as he sat down on the edge of the bed he lay back against it and was snoring before Raider had time to look around the place.

Raider lifted Manton's legs onto the bed, loosened the sleeping man's necktie, and let the poor SOB sleep. He needed it. Likely he would stay right where he was until morning.

It was early for supper, but the lunch on the train over from Albany had been about as filling as it was cheap—which was to say, neither of those—and he was hungry.

Besides, he wanted to get a look around this strange eastern town that was so smoky and busy and different from everything he was used to.

He went downstairs and passed by the hotel restaurant in search of something with a Yankee flavor to it.

Out on the streets of Hartford he wasn't sure he was still in the same country that had built San Francisco and Santa Fe and Cheyenne.

There wasn't a spur or a wide-brimmed hat in sight, and if a bunch of cowboys came larruping around a street corner with quirts in their hands and a gather of longhorn steers running in front of them, why, there would probably be a panic that'd topple buildings when these funny-dressed people tried to get out of the way.

Weird damned country, Raider decided. Folks didn't seem to speak to each other hardly at all. They passed each other on the streets without so much as a nod, much less a pleasant word, and most of them gave him funny, kind of suspicious looks.

He wondered what would happen if he made a face and shouted boo at somebody.

Probably shit their britches, he decided, and take half the population of the town with them when they legged it for the woods.

Woods. That was one thing they had enough of around here. Practically since the minute they crossed the Mississippi he'd felt hemmed in by trees and greenery. Like it all was pressing in on him and trying to choke him. He was used to country where a man could stand on a mountaintop —or in his own stirrups if that was the highest thing he had handy—and see to the horizon without laying an eye on anything much that was the result of man's presence.

Here a fella was lucky to be able to see across to the other side of the street. Most of the time he couldn't hardly do that, for there would be freight wagons or beer sledges or a mess of high-plumed ladies' hats in between him and whatever was on the other side of the street.

And the smoke? With all the factories and whatever, there were more chimneys right here in Hartford than you could probably find between the Rocky Mountains and the Pacific Ocean, and every one of those chimneys was busy pouring smoke and soot into the air. It practically hurt a man to breathe.

Raider realized he was probably being damned well uncharitable about all that, but the truth was that he was feeling out of place here. Like a foreigner almost. The quicker he could get back home—an area that covered roughly two-thirds of the continent—the better.

He found an eatery where the signboard outside advertised pot roast and thought he would try that. It sounded good after the cheap food he'd been sticking with for the benefit of Ted Manton's pocketbook.

It was good, too, but he was shocked by the price these people wanted for a simple meal. A dollar and ten cents for dinner and coffee, no dessert thrown in. He could have gotten the same meal in Cheyenne for forty cents. Raider guessed you had to be a rich man to make it here, although

the factory workers who were crowding the streets when he
left the restaurant didn't look all that rich. They looked
about as grimy and poorly dressed as hard-rock miners
coming off shift.

He pulled a splinter off a wood post and leaned against
the post to look things over a bit while he picked his teeth
with the splinter.

Next thing he knew both arms were pinioned behind
him, and a copper in a blue coat was threatening to break
his scalp open with a hickory stick.

"Don't move, damn you. Don't you be movin' a mus-
cle."

There was a distinct quaver of fear in the cop's voice.
"I'll bust your head if you move, mister."

The copper behind Raider emphasized the warning with
a painful tug on Raider's arms.

Raider's neck swelled with sudden fury, and for a moment he considered teaching these boys what-all they were
doing wrong. Neither of the idiots was armed except for
their sticks. One good stomp of a boot heel down the one's
shin and onto his foot, then a kick to the other one's cods
and . . .

"What the fuck's the matter with you two?" Raider demanded instead.

The one behind him pulled at his arms again, and the
one in front waved his stick in the air.

"Quit before you get me mad, damn it. Now what is this
about?"

The one with the stick squinted—Raider suspected the
cop likely believed the expression would make him look
fierce; to Raider it looked like the cop's eyes hurt—and
pointed toward the butt of the big Remington that rode at
Raider's waist. "An' what would ye be plannin' to do with
a cannon like that?"

"Planning? Hell, I'm not planning to do anything with it
unless somebody *plans* to do something to me first."

"A man don't carry a weepon like that wi'out a reason,
bucko. Now what is it you're up to?"

"What I am up to is having supper, which I just did, thank you. And I always carry a gun."

It seemed stupid as hell to Raider, but for some reason even the cops here didn't seem much for the carrying of guns.

"Think you're some kind o' desperado, do ye?"

"What I think I am is some kind of Pinkerton operative, you asshole, and if your partner doesn't leave go of my arms right about now I'm likely to get mad enough to stomp on the both of you. Now let go!"

The cop behind him did not completely let go, but there was a lessening of the pressure.

Raider shook himself free of the fellow and glared at both of them. "Are you people crazy, or what?"

"We've been getting complaints from folks on the streets. Sayin' there's a wild man with a big pistol runnin' loose."

"Jesus," Raider snorted. "Wild? You want to see wild, go see Telluride on a Saturday night. That's wild. Personally, I was just picking my teeth. And I haven't shot a single citizen of your town. Yet."

"You really a Pink?"

"Don't get excited. I'm gonna reach inside my coat for my wallet."

The cop nodded but looked nervous.

Raider showed his credentials and shook his head. "It's a sad damned thing when a man can't walk the streets without people getting excited about the sight of a revolver. Which by the way is what this is. It's a revolver, not a pistol. You do know the difference, don't you?"

The cops nodded, but Raider was not at all sure they were telling the truth.

"Look, mister," one of them said, "it'd be better really if you kept that thing out of sight here. This is a civilized city. No wild Indians in miles. You won't need a gun here."

"Huh! I've needed a gun with white men a damn site

more'n I ever have against Indians. Though I don't expect you to understand that either."

"You won't need it here," one of the cops said.

"Because you and your stick will be there to protect me day and night? Bullshit."

"How about if we ask you nicely. Please keep the pi . . . the revolver out of sight while you're here. Would you do that, please?"

Raider grunted unhappily, but he did comply to the extent of hitching his gunbelt higher and buttoning his coat so the holster could not be seen. "Is that better?"

"Yes, sir. Thank you."

The pair of coppers touched their hatbrims politely and went off down the crowded street with their billy clubs swinging.

Strange damned country, Raider thought again. He decided he needed a drink and the comforts of a friendly saloon to keep himself occupied. Otherwise he might go and get himself homesick. And for a man who really didn't have a home, that would be a helluva state of affairs.

Surely they had saloons here.

CHAPTER NINETEEN

The customers in the small, smoky place seemed to know each other and were friendly enough. But as a stranger in their midst, Raider might as well have not been there. The other men in the place stepped around him, talked around him, and looked through him. But no one ventured a hello. As a social highlight of his visit to the East, this wasn't doing much.

Raider finished off a single beer—that, at least, was plenty good—and motioned the bartender to him.

The man acted peeved to have to leave his conversation but came along and reached for Raider's empty mug.

Raider shook his head. "One's enough. I wanted to ask you where a stranger can find a good time in town."

A card game, a gambling house, just about anything would beat a saloon where everyone ignored him or a hotel room where the only person to talk to was sound asleep.

"Fifty cents," the bartender said. It seemed a poor answer to a pleasantly put question.

Raider thought about engaging in a lesson of manners, then decided it wasn't worth it. He handed over a half dollar, and the barman pocketed the coin.

"Two blocks down. The Blue Oyster. Second floor."

"Thanks." Raider got the hell out of the place and went down the street in the direction the bartender had pointed.

The Blue Oyster seemed like a repeat of the place he had just left except that the clientele was dressed better, and there was a staircase leading to a second floor. He ignored the bar and went upstairs. A door on the landing there was locked, and he had to knock to gain entry.

A peephole was opened but not the door, and an eye peered out at him.

"I don't know you, mister."

"Hell, nobody does in this town. A guy down the street told me to come here."

"You aren't a copper?"

"Why the hell would you care if I was?"

The eye looked him over, from Stetson to boots, and the door was pulled open. "You sure ain't from around here," the man said. He looked like a bouncer.

"That's the truth," Raider said with feeling.

The place was a whorehouse, and a shabby one at that. Nothing at all like a man could expect to find in Denver or San Francisco or New Orleans. It had all the warmth and charm of a meat-packing plant. It was still early, though, and the girl who quickly cuddled up to Raider's side was pretty enough.

"Aren't you the handsome one now," she said. She slipped an arm around his waist and recoiled slightly when she felt the hard steel of the Remington under his coat.

It occurred to Raider that as far as he could recall, hers was the first smile he had gotten since he got off the train that afternoon. And hers was of the bought-and-paid-for kind.

"Want a drink first, honey, or d'you just want to fuck?" she asked.

"How about a drink."

"Sure, honey. Out here or in my room?"

He looked at the poorly furnished parlor, half filled with people who were trying to pretend that they were alone. "In your room, I think."

"Whatever you say, honey." The girl led the way through a narrow, rabbit-warren hallway and into a tiny cubicle of a room that had no window and practically no furnishings. There was a cot, a lamp, and a washstand, nothing else.

"Five dollars, honey."

Raider lifted an eyebrow.

"It covers everything, honey, including your drink an' plenty of time to enjoy it." She winked. "An' whatever you want me to do for you."

Raider forked over a half eagle.

"Jeez, honey, we don't often see hard money."

Yet another of the many differences between here and what Raider was used to. On the good side of the big river, currency was the exception and coin the rule. Here that custom was apparently reversed.

"Be right back," the girl said. She left him alone in the room and returned a minute later with a single glass of whiskey and a smile.

While Raider tasted the whiskey—it wasn't nearly as good as the beer had been—she slipped quickly out of her dress and lay on the narrow cot.

With her clothes off she was not nearly as pretty as she had been when dressed. Her breasts were limp and sagging, and there was a livid scar on her belly just above her dark thatch of pubic hair. The vee, he noticed, was inky black although the hair on her head was a pale brass color.

Raider set the whiskey glass aside and lay down beside her.

The girl—he realized that she had neither given a name nor asked for one—reached over to fondle his crotch. He reacted with the beginnings of an erection.

"Um. Nice, honey. I like that."

She unbuttoned his fly and reached inside, kneading and clutching at him with a firm touch that was close to being painful.

"Take it easy," he said. "There's time enough to relax a little, isn't there?"

"Sure, honey, sure. But I'm a busy lady, y'know." She pronounced it lie-dee. "You wouldn't wanta keep the next guy waiting." For some reason she seemed to find that funny. At least she laughed. There was no real humor in her laughter and certainly no warmth in her touch.

Raider's cock went as limp as the whore's tits, and he pushed her hand away.

"Maybe this wasn't such a good idea after all," he said.

The whore seemed not at all offended, but her expression became hard and she said, "No refunds, honey. You don't want it, that's your problem. I don't give no refunds."

Raider bridled. Then began to grin. For the first time in a good many hours he was feeling genuinely amused. By this whole situation. By the entire eastern seaboard of the United States and, hell, as far as he knew on up into Canada too.

The hell with 'em. All of them. They liked their ways and were damned well entitled to them. Raider just happened to know of something better.

He sat up and drained off the whiskey remaining in the glass, then toasted the naked girl with the empty glass. "Thanks," he said.

She looked puzzled.

"This is probably the most expensive drink of whiskey I ever bought. But maybe I learned something from it, so I reckon I can't call it a waste. Thanks."

He bent to give her a quick, pleased kiss on the forehead and stood. He refastened the buttons of his fly, unbuttoned his coat, and settled his gunbelt down where it belonged.

Different, that's all this was. Certainly not better but in truth maybe not worse either. It was just different from what Raider was used to. And realizing that, he no longer felt so overwhelmed by the differences.

Nor, by damn, was he going to change himself any to accommodate what someone *else* thought was different.

"Thanks," he said and grinned, "honey."

He found his own way out and headed back toward the hotel and a good night's sleep.

CHAPTER TWENTY

Dwayne dabbed at his lips with a napkin and gave his host and hostess the warmth of his smile. "That was wonderful. Thank you."

Mrs. Clawson blushed prettily, obviously pleased. Her husband beamed at his wife. The meal truly had been a fine one. Roast pork with a thick gravy. Parsnips and corn fresh from the Clawsons' own garden. All of it topped off with a pear conserve.

Normally now the custom would be for the gentlemen to retire to the parlor for brandy and cigars. But not in this household. Neither of those vices would be appropriate here.

Ethel Clawson and Bessie cleared the table while young Bernard stayed, hoping to be able to listen in to the "grown-up" talk that would follow dinner.

"I can't tell you what a joy you've been to us this past week, Dwayne," the Reverend Clawson said. "All the help . . ."

Dwayne cut the preacher short with a blush and a lowering of his eyes. "Please, sir. It's you and your family who've been the joy. Being so far from home, why, this has been like finding a new and wonderful family for me."

"Shall we retire, Dwayne? This way. Bernard, I believe you have schoolwork to attend to."

"Aw, Dad!" The boy's protest was anguished.

"Hurry now. If you get it done in time you can come down and join us at the piano after."

The anguish disappeared from the child's expression and he scampered for the stairs.

Dwayne chuckled. "I suspect, sir, the schoolwork will be accomplished with more attention to speed than to diligence."

"Mmmph. You have a point there, Dwayne." With a sigh of contentment from the rich meal, the Reverend Clawson led Dwayne into a parlor that was dominated by an old but gleamingly polished spinet piano.

From the back of the house came the sounds of dishes being washed and frequently too the sounds of laughter.

"You have a lovely family, sir. Truly you do," Dwayne said with feeling. He meant every word of it.

"Thank you, lad. And I must say that already you seem very much a part of it, a welcome part I might add. Bernard idolizes you, you know."

"I'll try not to let him down, sir."

The Reverend Clawson waved the suggestion away and loosened the bottom buttons of his vest to free his belly from the constraint of the cloth. "You mentioned that you wanted to have a discussion with me, Dwayne. How can I help?"

"Apart from everything you've already done, you mean, sir?" Dwayne smiled and sat correctly upright.

"We've done nothing but enjoy your company, lad," Clawson assured him. "Now tell me. Do you have a problem? Something I might help with?"

"Not a problem, sir, but certainly something you might be able to help with." Dwayne looked down and blushed slightly. "As I already told you, sir, I've been taking time away from my studies because it occurred to me that I was laboring without a goal. Well, sir . . . in the past week or so I've been thinking. And I must admit that my thoughts have been influenced by your good works here, sir. By this opportunity to be with you and your family and to see firsthand the wonderful fruits of your labors, sir."

Clawson looked mildly pleased but also curious.

"You see, sir," Dwayne went on, "I've been thinking

that, when I get back to school that is, I might set my course toward a divinity degree, sir. With . . . and I hope I'm not being too presumptuous here . . . with the career goal of a youth ministry."

Clawson threw his head back and roared with pleasure. "Praise God, Dwayne. Thank you, Jesus."

"You don't . . . think it foolish of me, sir?"

"Foolish? My dear boy, there is nothing you could have said that would have made me happier. I can't think of anyone, not a single soul, I would rather see receive the call. Nor can I think of anyone better suited to the counsel of young people. I've seen for myself how boys and girls of all ages respond to you. With you to lead them, Dwayne . . ." He shook his head happily. "The possibilities are boundless."

"That is what I hope for, sir," Dwayne said solemnly.

The possibilities *would* be without limitation.

"You've made me very happy this evening, Dwayne. So happy I doubt I can convey it to you. But how can I help you, lad? You said something about asking a favor."

"Yes, sir, well . . . if you wouldn't mind, sir. I mean if it wouldn't be too much trouble . . ."

Clawson waved that silly idea away. Right at this moment there was practically nothing that would be too much for Dwayne Forbes to ask.

Practically nothing.

"What I was hoping, sir, would be, if you could see your way clear, that is, would be for you to write a letter of recommendation. I shall need something of the sort if I intend to change from liberal arts studies to a field of major study, particularly toward a divinity degree. And I was hoping also, sir, if it isn't too great a burden, that you might mark out for me a list. A reading guide, so to speak. I shall want to begin preparing before I return east, you see, and I thought if you were to give me a reading list . . ."

Clawson acted like the young gentleman had just paid him a great honor. "At once, Dwayne. I shall do so at once. And not only a list of reading materials, young man.

You shall be able to find most of the volumes in my library. Why, between the books I have here at home and those I keep at the church, son, we can provide you with nearly everything you require."

The preacher came to his feet, his excitement pulling his face into a wide grin. "I'll get you the first volumes now, Dwayne. And . . . may I have your permission to share this news with Mrs. Clawson and the children?"

"My permission, sir? Why, I certainly don't want to hide my light under a bushel. Please do tell them."

"They'll be as happy as I, Dwayne."

Clawson rushed out of the parlor, first to the kitchen to call his wife and daughter in, then to the foot of the staircase to call young Bernard down from his studies for the grand announcement.

Dish-washing and schoolbooks were abandoned, and the family gathered close around Dwayne, leading him to the piano with tears of laughter and proud, fond looks.

Reverend Clawson put an arm over Dwayne's shoulders and asked, "Tell us your favorite hymn, lad, and Elizabeth will play it for you."

Bessie looked up from the keyboard of the spinet with an exasperated smile. "Daddy, please! Nobody calls me that anymore."

CHAPTER TWENTY-ONE

Whoever this D. C. Florette was, he had some damned impressive surroundings. The 24 Cable Street address referred not to a house but to an office building. A *large* office building, occupying half the block on Cable between Post and Jackson.

What impressed Raider, though, was the carved marble slab above the main entrance to the huge building. The carving read: FLORETTE BUILDING, 1864.

"Damn," Raider said in admiration.

"Profiteers," Manton returned, his voice and expression sour.

"What's that?"

"I said the Florettes are likely war profiteers. Look at the date on the building, and then look around you at all the mills and factories here. It isn't so hard to guess, Raider. Ten to one—no, damn it, a hundred to one—the Florettes got their money from government contracts during the Rebellion. Probably some of those shrewd Yankees who paid to keep their own boys out of the conscript so they could stay home and make two-dollar uniforms that they sold to the government for twenty dollars. Lots of manufacturing up here then. Woolens and armaments and munitions. Plenty of profit but damned little blood."

Raider grunted something that could have been taken any way Manton wanted. He didn't want to open that old subject, particularly since it was pretty plain that Manton had strong feelings about it.

"One thing, Ted. When we get in to see this man, I want

you to keep yourself quiet. You understand me? You keep
your mouth closed or turn around right now and go back to
the hotel. Your daughter is dead. This man's son is still
alive. And even if the kid is the animal we think he is,
likely the father will want to protect him. D'you promise?"

Manton nodded. "I already said that I would, but—"

"No buts, Ted. Either you listen in quiet-like or I'll tell
you all about it afterward."

"I'll be quiet."

"Then let's go beard this lion."

A receptionist in the lobby of the imposing building directed them to the third floor, which was given over to an
elaborate set of offices. A second receptionist greeted them
there.

"Mr. D. C. Florette, please," Raider said.

"Have you an appointment?"

"Nope."

"Then I'm sorry, but you will have to make one." The
man opened a datebook and thumbed forward in it. "I can
give you an appointment with Mr. Florette's secretary on
Tuesday."

"With his secretary," Raider repeated. "On Tuesday."

"That is correct, sir."

"Sorry, bub, but that won't do. My business with Mr.
Florette is personal, confidential, and damned important."
He pulled out his Pinkerton credentials and displayed
them.

"I'm sure your business is most urgent," the receptionist
said smoothly, "but I have my orders. Do you want that
appointment or not?"

The receptionist was a scrawny sort with thinning hair
and the kind of pallor that said he never saw the sunshine
except through curtained windows. He didn't look strong
enough to lift a schooner of beer without help.

Raider leaned low over the man's desk so they were
face to face and said, "I didn't come three thousand miles
to play games, neighbor. And I'm not leaving here today,

right now, without seeing Florette. Do we understand each other?"

The receptionist turned his head and coughed uncomfortably. "I . . . it isn't possible for you to see Mr. Florette."

"Wanta bet?"

Raider's hand snapped up, and the receptionist flinched away from the expected blow. Instead Raider patted the man's cheek lightly, smiled, and started past him.

"But you can't . . ."

Raider ignored the yelp and sauntered down the main hall. On both sides were doors with frosted glass, each door neatly lettered with the name and title of the owner.

"Convenient," Raider mumbled to Ted Manton, who was dutifully following with, as promised, his mouth closed.

Manton pointed toward the end of the hall. The corridor terminated there at another frosted glass door, this one bearing the lettering: D. C. FLORETTE SR., PRESIDENT, CHAIRMAN OF THE BOARD.

"Uh huh. Convenient." Raider pushed the door open and let himself inside without knocking.

The office was smaller than he would have expected from the rest of the outfit. The single desk in it was cluttered and had a mechanical writing machine on a small table beside it. The man behind the desk was graying at the temples and had much more force of character than the receptionist out front.

"My name is Raider, from the Pinkerton National Detective Agency, and I need to have a word—" Raider began.

"Do you have an appointment?" the man interrupted.

"I won't need one. Not when you hear what I have to say." Raider glanced around. There were several men, businessmen from the look of them, seated in chairs ranked along the front walls. "But this is something I think you need to hear in private, Mr. Florette."

"I, sir, am Stanley Grenville, personal secretary to Mr. Florette. And if you have no appointment—"

"Oh." Raider pushed past this one too and started for a plain walnut door set in the back wall.

Grenville lunged forward to stop him, but Raider placed his palm over the secretary's face and shoved. Grenville pitched back into his chair with a gasp of outrage. "You can't—"

"Watch me," Raider growled.

The salesmen or buyers or whoever they were in the chairs looked away. None of them tried to interfere.

Raider stalked into D. C. Florette's private office, Ted Manton close behind him and a stammering Grenville immediately behind him.

"I tried to stop him, sir, but—" Grenville began.

"Shut up," Raider said. Stanley Grenville shut up.

"You." Raider pointed a finger at two men who were seated in leather-upholstered armchairs in front of a desk big enough to hold a baseball infield. He reversed his hand and jerked his thumb toward the door through which he had just barged. "Out."

They gaped at him.

"Now," he added.

They left, and a red-faced and uncomfortable Grenville followed them, choosing discretion over valor in this instance.

D. C. Florette Sr. had been watching the affair with interest but no apparent alarm.

"Sorry, but I needed to see you," Raider said, "and it isn't the sort of thing that can wait."

"So I gathered," Florette said in a dry voice.

Raider looked around the office. The thing was big enough. It probably included a quarter of the available square footage on this floor of the building.

The furnishings were big, fancy, and expensive. The walls were decorated with paintings that even to Raider's untrained eye looked old, fine, and extremely valuable. Much of one entire wall was devoted to windows overlooking the Connecticut River and the industrial plants that lined it.

This was what he might have expected.

D. C. Florette Sr., on the other hand, was *not* what he expected.

The man was well groomed, well dressed, handsome enough, with an air of money and power around him. That much, sure. What Raider had not anticipated was that Florette would be so old.

He was probably in his seventies, maybe more.

"You *are* D. C. Florette, aren't you?"

The old man inclined his head slightly.

"Like I said, I'm sorry for the intrusion. But I needed to speak with you about your son."

Florette frowned. "My son, you say?"

"That's correct." Once again Raider produced his credentials and identified himself.

Florette eyed them skeptically and said nothing when Raider helped himself to one of the recently vacated armchairs.

"Mr. Florette, it isn't my purpose to alarm you, but the Pinkerton Agency has reason to believe that your son may be in serious trouble, and—"

The old man gave Raider a bleak look and said, "My son, sir, has been gone these past five years."

"Yes, but we think we know where he is, or at least where he was recently, and we—"

"You misunderstand me, sir. *My son died five years ago.*"

CHAPTER TWENTY-TWO

There was a moment of shocked silence. Then Raider said, "I'm sorry, Mr. Florette. We didn't know."

"Quite a . . . surprise for me also, sir," Florette said. He sighed. "However, that being cleared up, I assume I can return to my normal routine now without further . . . disruption."

Raider glanced toward Manton, who was fidgeting on the edge of his seat and barely containing himself from speaking.

"Uh, as a matter of fact, Mr. Florette, I'm afraid it isn't all cleared up. If your son is dead, someone else must be using his name. And frankly, sir, I happen to have evidence that you are supplying that someone with funds."

Florette's expression hardened. "If this is your idea of a joke, sir . . ."

"It is not, I assure you. I have evidence, Mr. Florette, that you have sent funds, by way of Western Union bank draft, to a man sometimes known as Dane Florette and at other times known by other names—names under which he is wanted by the law in several different states and territories—such as Fallon and Fogarty."

"But Dane . . ." Florette had looked for a moment as if he was on the verge of anger. Then his face went slack with comprehension. "Dane? My . . . my grandson? In some kind of trouble?"

"Grandson?"

The old man—within those past few seconds he seemed to have withered; he looked actually smaller and older than

117

he had when Raider and Manton burst in on him a few minutes earlier—slumped in his chair.

"My..." He was trembling now. "It is simple, really. I am Dane Carlton Florette Sr. My son was Dane Carlton Florette Jr. The ... the boy, my son's boy, is Dane Carlton Florette III. You ... say he may be in some sort of trouble, sir?"

"I'm sorry to say it, but yes. We ... the Pinkertons ... have reason to believe your grandson may be in serious trouble."

"I suppose I should be surprised. I rather wish I could be. I'm afraid, however, that I can't. He ... surely he can't have stolen anything. I've tried to meet my obligations to ... to my son. In his memory, so to speak. Although the boy and I never got along too well. We never saw eye to eye on much of anything. But ... if anything has been stolen, sir, I shall of course make restitution to the ... aggrieved parties. Whatever it takes. I ... haven't much, sir, but I do have money. At least I do have quite a lot of money."

Raider gave Manton a look of warning, then said, "I'm afraid it isn't the sort of thing where money could compensate, Mr. Florette."

"What has the boy done?"

"*If* we are correct," Raider said, stressing the *if*, "your grandson has committed murder, Mr. Florette. On several different occasions."

"Murder!" It came out in a gasp. "But ... that cannot be possible. No Florette has ever..." His voice broke, and it took him a moment to recover. "Ours is a proud family, Mr. Raider. A proud and respectable family. Surely you must be mistaken about these ... these outrageous charges. I cannot believe that any Florette would ever..." His back straightened and his jaw firmed. "I believe you should speak with my attorney if you wish further information from me, Mr. Raider. I really believe that would be the best course of action. He will, I am certain, clear this up quite readily."

Manton had been edging further and further forward on his chair. Now he came to his feet before Raider could stop him.

"You sanctimonious old son of a bitch," Manton burst out. "Your grandson killed my daughter. Murdered her in cold blood. Raped her first and then murdered her. And went on to rape and murder more innocent girls. All across this country, in Missouri and California and Washington and in California again, and—"

"Stanley. Stanley!" Florette shouted.

Raider pulled Manton back from the desk and shoved him down into his chair.

The secretary threw the door open with alarm at the old man's outcry.

"Have someone sent up to throw these men out, Stanley," Florette ordered.

"Mr. Florette, we need your help," Raider pleaded. "We need you to help us stop Dane from killing again."

"Get out. Get out, I say. I shall listen to no more of this nonsense."

A young man, dressed for office work but burly enough, rushed in and tried to grapple with Ted Manton. It was probably a good choice. Manton was half Raider's size. Raider grabbed him by the neck and threw him aside. That prompted Manton to go for Florette, although what he intended to do with the old fellow Raider couldn't guess. For that matter, Manton probably didn't know himself. He just wanted to do something. Anything.

"Will you please calm the fuck down and listen to reason?" Raider roared.

Two more office workers ran in, bent on throwing out the intruders. Raider stopped the first of them with a hard, chopping right hand. The second man tried to kick Raider in the balls.

"Your rules, mister," Raider said and dropped him with a much better aimed boot toe.

The one who had gone for Manton was back on his feet and charging forward with courage if not with skill. Raider punched him in the throat and had to deal a second time with the other man he had hit. The one he had kicked in the cods looked like he wasn't going to be interested in anything outside himself for quite some time to come.

"Damn it, Florette, you've got to listen. You're putting young girls' lives on the line."

There was a mad pounding of footsteps on a distant staircase, and a moment later a swarm of more Florette employees poured into the office. There were six, ten . . . Raider quit trying to count them and concentrated on trying to keep them off of Ted Manton, who had fallen to the floor and was slumped against the front of D. C. Florette's desk. He looked gray and clammy, and Raider was afraid he was having a heart attack.

Florette did not look to be in such great shape either. He had retreated to the wall of windows and was standing with his back to them, his face drawn, his color nearly as bad as Manton's.

Raider ducked under a wildly inexpert punch, turned the puncher's face into a mask of blood with a powerful left hook, and felt his knees buckle as someone tackled him from behind.

Raider kicked out blindly at whoever had him and was rewarded with a screech of pain. But there was another to take that man's place and another to replace the replacement, and more of them were still streaming through the boss's door.

Short of hauling out the Remington and depopulating the Florette Building there just wasn't much Raider could do about it. There were simply too many of them.

"Damn it, Florette, you listen to me," he barked as hands clawed at him, turning him over and pulling him toward the door.

"You've got to tell us where that bastard Dane is!" On an impulse—he had no idea where it came from—he added, "You've got to tell us about Elizabeth!"

Half a dozen angry men were carrying him bodily toward the door, but across the room he could see Florette stiffen. The old man's pallor deepened, and a hand came up across his eyes.

"Wait!" Florette snapped. "What . . . did you say?"

The men carrying Raider stopped. They did not release him, but they stopped at their employer's command.

"I said, in the name of decency, man, you have to tell us about Elizabeth. Innocent lives depend on it."

Again the name took effect on the old man. Florette staggered and had to grab the back of his desk chair to support himself or he would have fallen.

"That slut," he whispered. "What does she have to do with this?"

"That's what we're begging you to tell us," Raider said, squirming against the hands that bound him.

"Jezebel," Florette hissed. "Delilah."

Florette fell into his chair more than sat in it. He buried his face in both hands.

"Put me down now," Raider ordered quietly.

Incredibly, the men did.

Raider extracted Manton from the two men who had been hauling him off. He motioned for the employees to leave the room and assisted Manton back to the armchair.

"Whore," Florette mumbled.

Raider shooed the last of the men out of the office and pushed Stanley Grenville out behind them. Then he returned to face D. C. Florette.

"Tell us about Dane and Elizabeth," he said softly.

CHAPTER TWENTY-THREE

Dwayne Forbes looked up from his book at the sound of approaching footsteps. The study was difficult but interesting, and Reverend Clawson's suggestions were even more helpful than Dwayne had hoped.

Clawson expected Dwayne to use the knowledge gained here as a spur for his education. In fact, Dwayne had no such intent. The studies Clawson was being so helpful with would serve him *instead* of a formal degree in the subject.

With a little imagination and the assistance of a forger —available nearly anywhere for a mere pittance—he would soon be able to convince anyone that he held a bachelor's degree in divinity and was well along in a master's program as well.

It was ideal, he realized.

And best of all, Dwayne Forbes was practically a member of the Clawson household by now.

Each afternoon he joined the Reverend Clawson at the church for an hour of study there. Then the two of them walked together to the Clawson home, where Dwayne normally took his supper *with the family* and then stayed afterward to study in the preacher's well-stocked personal library.

It couldn't have been more perfect.

He was already smiling, having recognized her footsteps, when Bessie appeared at the sliding double doors to the library and gave him a shy smile.

She was really a fetching child, this Elizabeth Henrietta Clawson.

Very young, of course.

That had actually bothered Dwayne at first. He hadn't been sure if a girl so very young—she was not quite fifteen yet—was a proper candidate for the help he could give her.

Then he realized the truth.

Of course she was a proper candidate for his guidance.

Once he really thought about it, Dwayne realized that he was being guided in this.

Always before the Jezebels had been delivered to him after an age of flirtatiousness. Sixteen, eighteen, as old as twenty-six that immature young woman in Savannah had been.

Always before, his help had come barely in time to give them the salvation they so desperately needed.

But now, with Bessie, he would be able to save her even from the *contemplation* of fleshly sin.

That knowledge had been a true revelation for him.

It opened up a whole new field of candidates to him.

Particularly in light of the opportunities Clawson was giving him.

As an ordained minister himself specializing in the counsel of youth—this knowledge and a piece of sheepskin would make that so—he would be able to see to the needs of limitless young women and younger girls. Positively limitless.

Thinking about this, the smile he gave Bessie Clawson held a warmth that was genuine clear to the core of Dane Florette's being.

"Am I bothering you?" she asked hesitantly.

"Dear Bessie. You couldn't be a bother to me if you tried," he said quite honestly.

She blushed. Bernard had begun to idolize Dwayne almost from the beginning, flattered and excited that a near-grown-up would seriously pay attention to the nine-year-old's conversation. It was becoming clear to all of them, to Dwayne and her parents alike, that Bessie too had fallen under Dwayne's charm. The Reverend and Mrs.

Clawson were amused by their daughter's first crush on an "older man." They even gently encouraged it.

Just last night, after the children were abed, the Reverend Clawson had mentioned it to Dwayne.

"I hope you don't mind Elizabeth's infatuation," he had said.

"Mind? I'm flattered, sir. Bessie is a lovely child. So bright and pretty and full of life. I enjoy her thoroughly."

"I'm glad, lad. Frankly, Ethel and I have been worried about her. She is, as you say, quite pretty, for which I give her mother full credit, certainly not myself." He laughed. "She's nearing that age when she will be thinking about boys, you know, and one can never be sure of the youngsters in a public school. Even the ones here, excellent though they are. So we are really quite pleased to see her primp and preen on your behalf and not for some wild young ruffian. Ethel and I have talked about that, you see, and neither of us can think of any young man finer or more sensible than yourself, Dwayne. No, don't pretend to a modesty that is quite ill deserved, young man. It's the truth. If we have any regrets it would be that there is such a difference in your ages. Why, if Elizabeth were a little older or you a few years younger, we would be encouraging our daughter to set her cap for you, Dwayne."

"I hardly know what to say to that, sir. Thank you."

"We mean it, Dwayne. Most sincerely. And we feel confident that our Elizabeth couldn't be in better hands than yours during this difficult time of growth toward maturity."

"You have my word, sir, that I shall do everything I can to insure that Bessie remains pure and true for all eternity," Dwayne had told Bessie's father with feeling.

"I know you will, lad. We both know it, or you and I shouldn't be having this little talk, eh?"

Now Bessie blushed, mercifully unaware that her innermost thoughts and yearnings were open knowledge, and raised her eyes shyly to meet Dwayne's. "I know you're busy studying, but Mama let me bake a pan of oatmeal cookies. They're just out of the oven, and I thought . . . I mean if you . . ."

Dwayne gave the child a brotherly smile. "You baked them yourself?"

She nodded while she examined the scuffed toes of her shoes protruding under the edge of her skirts.

"Then I should certainly like to try them."

"They might not be any good, actually. And I know you're busy."

"Never too busy for a fresh-baked cookie. Especially from the hands of such a pretty girl."

Bessie blushed quite furiously at that, which Dwayne pretended not to notice.

"Besides," he said, "you caught me at just the right time. I was just stretching."

"Good," she said, pleased but too shy to look at him directly. "We could have them in the kitchen."

"Perfect."

"I'll tell Bernard. But don't worry. I . . . I'll make sure you get the nicest ones." She turned in a swirl of skirts and dashed off down the hall, leaving an amused Dwayne behind.

And, he would have admitted to no one but himself, an aroused Dwayne as well.

He could feel the excitement of anticipation tingle deliciously in his groin when the swish of Bessie's hem showed her ankles and a calf well above the tops of her shoes.

He certainly hadn't been lying to Reverend Clawson when he said that Bessie—Elizabeth—was an uncommonly pretty child.

She was breathtakingly lovely.

And so innocent.

It was such a pity that such innocence and purity must inevitably be defiled and destroyed by the worldly vices.

But not, praise God, in dear Bessie's case.

Dane Florette would see to that.

Dane would preserve her from that. Dane would show

her the error of sin and grant her the salvation she needed so.

Dwayne sat where he was for a moment, staring down at the book open on the reading table before him, until his erection subsided.

Then, with real love in his heart for this entire, wonderful family, he went back to the kitchen to join them in praising Bessie's cookies.

CHAPTER TWENTY-FOUR

There was a tall ebony sideboard in the room that was covered with fancy glasses and even fancier decanters, each of them labeled with engraved brass tags to show what kind of hooch was in them. Raider poured glasses of brandy for Ted Manton—who still looked like hell after the excitement—and for Florette—who didn't look a whole hell of a lot better.

"Drink those and calm down a minute," Raider told them. He went back to the bar and helped himself to a jolt of Florette's bourbon.

The old man recovered his coloring fairly quickly, but it took Manton a second glass of the brandy to get back to something approaching normal. When Manton looked to be breathing easily again Raider slouched in the armchair facing Florette and said, "I believe you were going to tell us about Elizabeth?"

Instead of answering, the aging businessman asked, "Is that slut still alive? How in the world did the boy ever find her? What . . . are the two of them together now?"

Raider hid his own ignorance in a frown. "First you tell us about them. Both of them. Then we'll give you what we know."

Florette did not look happy about it, but at least he didn't call for help again. Raider was agreeable to that. The knuckles on his right hand stung like hell from hitting somebody, and come tomorrow he would be feeling the bruises that swarm of office workers had inflicted on him.

The old man took his time about it, hemming and hawing and staring out the window for a while first. Finally he spoke.

"I tried to tell my son not to marry that woman in the first place. She wasn't our sort. Not . . . quality."

Right, Raider thought sourly. Not quality like little ol' Dane the Third. Sure. But he said nothing.

"She was an actress, you see. At least that is what she called herself. Saloon bawd is more like it, but the boy wouldn't listen to me. Said he was in love with her and was determined to marry her even if I disowned him, which I threatened to do but . . . couldn't. Not when it came right down to it. My only child. Not just my heir but my son. Can you understand what that means? He was my son." Florette looked miserable.

Raider shot a glance toward Ted Manton. Manton understood, all right. Manton had never had a son, but he once had had a daughter. This white-haired old man's grandson had taken that daughter from him. Dane Florette Sr. had had a choice about his child that was denied to Ted Manton. Manton's expression showed understanding but no sympathy.

"The marriage was a mistake, of course. As I had predicted. Actually it lasted longer than I expected. The boy was twelve when Elizabeth . . . left." He coughed, and his face twisted with some emotion that Raider could not read. Not just disapproval. Not just hate. There was something more as well.

"Left, you say?" Raider pressed, not wanting Florette to gloss over whatever that particular memory was.

Florette gave him a nervous look. "You. . . . probably read about it. The scandal," he said.

"I don't think so," Raider said politely, deciding not to add that small scandals in an unimportant corner of the world like Connecticut were not likely to make the headlines in Montana or Arizona or wherever Raider might have been those years ago when, as he was beginning to suspect, the Florette family was disgraced.

"It . . . was unpleasant. Elizabeth was undeniably pretty.

She still looked quite young. I suppose she thought herself
. . . bored with her life here. Or some such excuse. But
that, of course, is speculation. I neither know nor care
what the Jezebel's reasoning was. The fact is . . . the fact is,
with her husband's concurrence, she had become quite
heavily involved in matters of the church. As was the boy
at the time. Quite active, both of them. She took the boy to
every possible function or affair and was herself involved
in the choir and certain charitable works.

"What . . . what no one in the family realized at the time
was that her supposed church activities were really an excuse for her to leave the house. Her Sunday piety was
meant to hide a sinful, lustful heart. She . . . actually engaged in lewd behavior . . . inside the sanctuary itself, as it
turned out . . . with the choir director, with certain other
members of the adult choir, even with several of the older
boys of the youth choir. It was . . . disgusting." The old
man had not looked in Raider's direction since he began
speaking. Now he buried his face in his hands again.

"The boy, my grandson, discovered his mother's . . .
indiscretions. By accident. He was searching for a piece of
sheet music the organist requested. He . . . walked unannounced into the choir director's office. His mother was
there. She was . . . naked. As were the choir director and
another church member. All of them naked. All of them
. . . lasciviously engaged in vile fornication. All three of
them at, uh, once."

Florette looked so upset by the memory that Raider
wondered about the breadth of the old fellow's own experiences. Limited, most likely. Straitlaced.

"The boy was . . . shocked. Devastated. He . . . thought
the two men were attacking his mother. Hurting her. He
screamed for help and ran to her assistance. He tried to
fight with the men. Naturally his screams aroused attention. It was . . . awful. Truly awful. That whore naked in
the office with the two men. The crying, frightened child.
The realization when others arrived. There was talk, of
course. We . . . I . . . tried to keep it quiet. That was not pos-

sible. The choir director was discharged in disgrace, of course. The . . . other male member of the congregation at least had the decency to put a bullet through his own head afterward. There was . . . considerable attention paid to it in the newspapers." Florette's voice faltered.

Raider was beginning to be able to see some sense in the story now. The mother Elizabeth seen so graphically as a Jezebel, as Florette kept calling her. The boy's horror and disgust, probably ingrained into him for years afterward by this puritanical old man, turned now against every Elizabeth in the stead of the one real Elizabeth who had defiled herself before his young eyes. It was crazy as hell maybe, but it made sense in a crazy as hell kind of way.

"What about Elizabeth?" Raider asked.

"Dane, my son Dane Junior, was out of town that evening. He was supposed to be away on business. He told me afterward, in a moment of grief, that he was actually in New Britain having a liaison with another woman. Because of that, I suppose, he felt a degree of guilt himself. A desire for forgiveness. But of course the whore, the Jezebel, had gone far beyond forgiveness. The scandal was . . . insurmountable. Not that I can understand Dane's desire for reconciliation anyway. I advised him against it. Strongly."

I'll just bet you did, Raider thought to himself.

"The culmination of it all, more than a week afterward, after the public display of it had been in the shoddier newspapers, was an argument, a very loud and unpleasant scene, in our family home. Dane—the boy, that is—overheard. We hadn't any idea that he was still awake and had come downstairs. He heard all of it. It only served to add to his distress. Affected him for years afterward, actually. Although of course there was no way we could have anticipated that at the time. Nor, frankly, would I have changed anything if I had had that insight and that power. There really was no choice in the matter. The entire family was disgraced. Our position would have been utterly ruined had my son granted the vile creature forgiveness and allowed her to remain. He saw that, of course. So did she. She was given a sum of money and sent away on the promise that she would contact none of our family ever again, the boy in particular. Nor, to the best of my knowledge, has she. Unless of course your information . . ."

Raider ignored the implied question and pressed Florette. "You said the boy suffered effects of this, uh, incident for some time afterward. What was that all about?"

Now that the worst of it was over, Florette looked at Raider again. "It was only a temporary thing."

"Tell me about it."

"A drink first?"

The old man was stalling. "Sure," Raider said.

Florette refilled all three men's glasses and took his time about settling into his chair again.

"The boy was essentially motherless afterward, of course. And my son continued to be fully occupied by his, our, work. All the busier, if anything. And I had only so much time to spend with the boy, although I did devote as much time as possible to his well-being and education. Still, he seemed deeply upset by the . . . troubles. Nervous. Excessively pious for a time, then almost abusive of anything relating to the church. Frequently ill. With Dane gone so much of the time, I felt it wise to send him away to school. I chose an institution well known for its, um, counseling services. Its abilities to reach and to discipline . . . problem youngsters. Not that the boy was a problem himself, you understand. It was that he had problems. So we sent him to this school. A very fine institution. And he remained there, doing quite well according to all reports, until his father's untimely death."

"That was five years ago, you said?"

"Yes, and unfortunately it was the boy who once again was the discoverer of disaster."

"Disaster."

"Terrible. Untimely, of course. As any father would believe after being forced to outlive his only child."

Raider glanced at Manton, but he was concentrating on his drink and kept quiet still.

"The boy was returning home for the Christmas holiday. He had gotten away a day early, so none of us knew to send a coach to the depot for him. Things . . . things might have been different, so different, had he wired ahead, had his father gone to meet him. In the event, however, the boy came home unannounced. He dawdled at the railroad depot, talking with someone there. He berated himself terribly for that afterward. Had he come home immediately upon leaving the train . . . But never mind that. Can't be changed now, of course." The old man took a deep breath.

"The house was in flames. Deliberate arson, as was proven by the authorities afterward. They believe it to have been the work of an intruder. A thief. My . . . my son was murdered. With his own handgun. It was discovered near his body. And . . . uh . . . and the body of a woman. Unidentified. She never has been identified to this day. She was quite badly consumed by the flames, you see. The arsonist set the fire, apparently, immediately at the body of the woman who was . . . in Dane's bed. My son . . . my son's body was nearby. And the weapon near him. Both had been shot to death before the fire was set. Again there was ugly rumor amounting to scandal. One newspaper went so far as to drag up the old scandal of that woman's conduct and speculated that it was she who died without identification in the burnt ruins of my son's home. They claimed she had been seen in town, at the railroad depot, the previous day. A holiday homecoming by the fallen woman, they claimed. That was nonsense, of course. They only did it to sell their filthy newspapers. And to hurt me. The simple fact was, of course, that Dane had some trollop in to . . . ease his physical needs. Nothing more than that. It was only chance that placed the two of them in the path of a murderous sneak thief."

"What did this thief steal?" Raider asked.

"Whyever would that be of interest to you?"

Raider shrugged. "A detective's curiosity."

Florette frowned but said, "Actually, it was never determined what was taken. My son's home was decorated with valuable art collectibles, just as this office is. He... derived his appreciation for the arts from me. And, too, his knowledge of the appreciable value of such pleasures. Naturally, in the aftermath of a fire, it is not always possible to determine what was stolen or what may have been consumed by the flames. The insurance company questioned the loss, but as we, Dane that is, was covered for both theft and fire loss, the point was dropped and the claim adjusted satisfactorily."

Adjusted satisfactorily? Raider was willing to bet that that meant the insurance paid off for more than the purchase price of the paintings. The shrewd old Yankee fart had actually turned a profit on his son's death.

"And you say the boy discovered this, too?"

"Sad to say, yes. He returned home in time to discover the fire already established on the upper floors. He rushed to turn in the alarm, of course, but by then it was much too late for the fire company to do more than to contain the blaze and keep it from spreading to other structures. Not that there were any other homes near, but the stables and summer house were in jeopardy. The fire company was able to save those from destruction. The... true extent of the loss, my son's body, was not discovered until the second day, when the embers cooled and it was safe for the authorities to investigate closely."

"This whole thing must have been terrible for you, Mr. Florette."

"You can't possibly know."

"I can," Manton said. "Because of what that boy Dane did to my daughter, damn you all."

"Hush, Ted," Raider said quickly.

Florette looked like Manton had just struck him. "Please. You must understand..."

"No, damn it, you're the one who has to understand. That grandson of yours is going around the country murdering innocent young girls. Any of them who happen to

be named Elizabeth. Like my child. Like my poor dead
Liz." Manton broke down and began to cry.

"I . . . surely you understand that I find this most difficult to believe," Florette said.

"Believe it," Raider said softly. "It's sorry news we
bring you, Mr. Florette, but that happens to be the truth.
Your grandson kills innocent girls, and so far all of them
have been named Elizabeth."

"Dear God," Florette whispered. "Can this be?"

CHAPTER TWENTY-FIVE

The old man looked haggard, nearly as bad as Ted Manton had become in recent days and weeks. And that was very bad indeed. His hand shook as he raised his glass of brandy to thin, age-puckered lips, and he drank the fluid like a medicine rather than a pleasure.

"Is there anything I can do for you, Mr. Florette?" Raider asked. Manton was being quietly hostile with the killer's grandfather, but Raider wanted him for an ally, not an enemy, in this search for Dane Florette III.

"No. No, I just . . . this is hard to credit, Mr. Raider. Very hard."

"I understand, sir, but the facts are plain enough."

Raider patiently went through it all again.

The deaths they knew about. The girls in Kansas City, San Francisco, Olympia, and Fresno.

The dead sheriff's daughter and her story about the man she knew as Fogarty replenishing his funds. The Western Union records showing that in that same time period Dane Florette III had received a telegraphed bank draft from D. C. Florette.

The old man nodded at that point. "I do remember sending Dane the money, of course. He . . . requests funding often. Large amounts."

"What does he say he wants the money for, Mr. Florette?"

"He . . . Dane and I are not close. Never have been, really. I suppose the fact is that I resent him for living when my son has died. And of course I never did approve of his

135

mother. He knows that. At one point, after his mother's public disgrace, the boy and my son lived with me. Under my roof, you see. It was an uncomfortable period for Dane. My son Dane, that is. I wanted to be of help. For a while there I thought I was able to exert some influence over the boy. But he has always been . . . different. Not bad, you understand. Not even really difficult. Just . . . different. Withdrawn. Not one to display his true feelings, whatever they may have been. Then, of course, he was sent away to school. And I thought they were making such progress with him. But then the . . . the fire. The loss of his father. The . . . awkwardness of discovering that there was a woman in the bedroom with Dane. For some reason that seemed to quite shock the boy, although he never discussed it with me at any great length. He withdrew then to the point of being actually sullen at times. He refused to return to school afterward. I made an effort to bring him into the business, but he was openly hostile to that. We . . . quarreled. Bitterly, I am afraid. It was almost as if he was accusing me of the tragedies our family suffered. And he left. I told him I would meet my obligations to him. As I mentioned to you before, I do have money. Nothing else, I'm afraid, but I do have money." Florette looked down at his gnarled, trembling hands.

"How often does Dane ask you for money?" Raider asked.

"No regular schedule, of course. Now and then I receive a wire from some distant place or other. I respond, as you already know, with a bank draft. Sometimes not for the full amount he asks. I do wish he would learn some responsibility, you know. Come to learn the value of hard work and money alike."

Raider nodded. Judging from what he had seen in the Western Union records, this old man's idea of prudence was hardly in line with what a working man's notions on that subject might be. Florette seemed willing enough to send off a draft for enough money to keep a normal family in tall cotton for eight or ten years yet thought it little enough to encourage prudence.

Still, it was probably all a matter of viewpoint. The Florette family resources seemed limitless from Raider's position. To one of them, though, three or four thousand dollars probably *was* very little.

"Have you heard from him recently?"

"Since I sent the funds to Olympia?"

Raider nodded.

"Once. As a matter of fact, and I know what you will be thinking about it, as perhaps you should, only a few weeks after that. The wire, if I remember correctly, came that time from a smallish town in the south of Washington. I don't recall the name. Something quite odd and unpronounceable. I could look it up if it is important."

Raider shook his head. There was no need for that. The Fresno murder had proven already that Dane Florette had not run for Canada after murdering Sheriff Simmons and Howard Turley. "Did he give any reason for asking for so much again so soon?"

"As a matter of fact he did, although that was not . . . is not, I mean . . . usual. He included in his wire mention of being fleeced at cards."

Raider grunted. "The fact, of course, is that his money was lost when that wagon ran off with the two dead men in it."

Florette nodded unhappily.

"Does he write to you, Mr. Florette? Have you any idea where he might be now?"

"He doesn't write," the old man said. "He only wires when he needs money, and he never writes to me."

"I can't say that I'm surprised," Raider mused. "It would be awkward for him trying to collect mail under his real name when he is posing under other names. Tough enough using the telegraph under those circumstances. Probably he prefers to send his wires from cities where he is not . . . planning another murder. His pattern about that is certainly clear enough. He always uses a false name and always poses as a pious young man when he is winning the confidence of his victims."

"That part at least is certainly true to his character. Dane has always been fuzzy-minded on the subject of religion. Particularly since the . . . experience with his mother. It was like he was . . . trying to compensate, somehow. To make up for her sinfulness."

"Correct me if I'm wrong," Raider said dryly, "but I think murder is mentioned in one of the Commandments."

"I make no claims to a religious bent myself, Mr. Raider. But yes. I see your point. It doesn't make sense, does it?"

Raider shrugged. "That's one of the things an investigator learns, Mr. Florette. The things that're logical and reasonable to a normal person just don't look the same to a . . . excuse me, but the conclusion is inescapable . . . to a crazy person. I'm sorry to say this, Mr. Florette, but I think your grandson has gone round the bend. So we aren't necessarily looking for things that would seem right or wrong to you and me. We have to remember that Dane is working under his own views of right and wrong. And those things just might not be what we would recognize at all."

Florette sank even lower into his chair, as if the weight of it all was pressing down on him heavier and heavier until he could no longer hold up on it.

Raider leaned forward and touched the old man on the wrist. Florette could not have known it—for that matter probably not Ted Manton either—but *this* was what Raider had really come all the way to Connecticut to accomplish.

"Mr. Florette," he said gently. "We need your help. Dane needs your help. He is a sick young man, Mr. Florette. He needs help. And all those innocent young girls named Elizabeth need help too. They need protection from Dane, and Dane needs to be treated somehow. I don't really know what all could be done to help him. Maybe you know more'n I do about that. But I do know that the boy has to be stopped. He has to be found and put someplace where he can get the help he needs an' can't hurt anybody else while he's doing it, Mr. Florette. For his own sake an' your family's sake an' for the sake of all those girls he might yet kill if he isn't stopped. And for the dead girls that he's already killed, like Mr. Manton's daughter Liz. He has to be stopped, sir. And we need your help to stop him."

Florette gave Raider an anguished look and lowered his eyes.

Manton, apparently realizing now what Raider was trying to do, leaned forward also. "Your grandson has destroyed my family, Mr. Florette. I don't want to think he will be free to destroy others as well." Manton paused for a moment. "Including yours, Mr. Florette."

"What do you want me to do?" the old man asked.

Florette was staring painfully down toward his hands, so he did not see the small smile that played on Raider's lips.

CHAPTER TWENTY-SIX

"You've a quick mind, Dwayne."

"Thank you, sir," Dwayne said with a smile.

The Reverend Mr. Clawson searched the shelving and brought down another volume, this one slender and poorly bound, its varnished cloth cover and spine showing the results of much use. "This one," he said, "was a favorite of mine when I was in school myself. I haven't had much need for it lately, but I think it may be of interest to you."

He handed the book to Dwayne and picked up the much heavier tome Dwayne had just finished, returning it to its place on the shelves. "Besides," he said, "this one is lighter reading. You push yourself terribly hard, Dwayne. You really should relax more. Enjoy yourself a little."

"I really don't find the study a burden, sir. Indeed, it is quite exciting."

Clawson smiled. "Exactly the way I felt about it when I was your age, dear boy."

They were interrupted by footsteps hurrying through the empty sanctuary. It was evening, and Dwayne and Clawson were alone in the church. Or at least Dwayne had thought they were.

"Bessie. What is it, dear?"

The child was out of breath. She paused at the door for a moment to recover, then said, "It's Mrs. Turner, Daddy. Dr. Mason sent word that you should come."

"She's at home?"

Bessie nodded. "Dr. Mason said there's no point in trying to get her to the hospital. Better to let her slip away with her family around her."

The preacher nodded. He reached for his hat and snugged his tie tight against his collar. "Tell your mother I'll be home when I can, but she's not to wait dinner for me. Or wait up for me, for that matter. One never knows how long these things can take."

"Is there anything I can do, sir?" Dwayne asked quickly. The concern and sincerity in his voice and expression were feigned. He had met Mrs. Turner. The woman was a shrill old bitch, and she was ancient. It would be not great loss when she died.

"No, Dwayne, thank you." Clawson headed for the door. "Come to think of it, there is. Would you see Bessie safely home, please? And stay to dinner, of course." He smiled. "Our table would seem empty without you, lad." He made no mention of his own probable absence from that table tonight. Things like this were one of the things he had been called to do.

"Of course, sir."

"Good." Clawson nodded a fond goodbye to his protégé and bent to give Bessie a quick kiss on top of her head, then hurried away. Dwayne could hear his footsteps echo as they receded through the dim, cavernous emptiness of the big church.

Then there was the slam of the front doors, and Dwayne was alone in the church with Bessie.

Bessie puffed her cheeks out and made a mock showing of wiping imaginary sweat from her pretty brow. Then she went behind her father's desk and plopped into his chair with a flounce of ruffles and crinolines. "Whew! I'm bushed. I practically ran the whole way." She grinned at him.

Dwayne stood. He was at the side of the small room, at the battered little desk that Clawson had installed for him there.

"Give me a minute to rest, please?" Bessie asked. "Besides, I don't want to interrupt your studies." She added an impish grin and said, "If I get back right away, I'll have to set the table. If we stay and let you study a little while more, Bernard will have to do it."

Dwayne laughed. "Then by all means we shall stay, Elizabeth."

Bessie cocked her head to one side and nibbled at her underlip. Her lips, he noticed, were rather full and pretty for a girl so young. "Can I ask you something?"

"Of course. Anything at all."

"Why do you call me Elizabeth? The rest of the family calls me Bessie."

"But most of your friends call you Elizabeth," he countered. "Aren't we friends, Elizabeth?"

She giggled. "Gosh, I guess so. I mean I . . . I'd like for us to be. I've never had a friend who's so . . . grown-up. You know? Mama says I should think of you like a big brother, sort of. But I'd like for us to be friends, too."

"So would I." He smiled. "Besides, you're much too grown up yourself to take on any new brothers. Particularly brothers older than you."

Bessie giggled again. She also sat up straighter in her father's chair as if she had suddenly become conscious that she was indeed growing up herself. Probably that was the first time in her life that anyone had intimated that she was in the process of becoming a grown-up.

With her posture so rigidly upright like that, Dwayne could see that she was not quite completely flat of chest.

There was a delicious little rosebud swell of breast beneath the bodice of her dress. Dwayne smiled and inspected her more closely, allowing himself now to openly assess her. The small, unformed shape of her. The curve of her eyelashes over the smooth softness of her cheeks. The delicate shape of her nose and chin. The slenderness of her neck.

And of course the tender vulnerability of her throat.

He could see the very spot. High on the left side of her neck, just beneath the softly rounded jaw shelf. Just below her ear.

He felt the stir of lust—no, damn it, of compassion—as he looked at her.

He wanted to *save* her from the sins of the world, not to harm her.

What he felt for her was love. A deeper and truer love than most girls could ever hope to experience.

What he felt for her was good and cleansing and sweet.

The salvation he had to offer her was, after all, for her own benefit and not his.

His smile became even gentler and truer.

She could have read nothing in Dwayne's expression—he had excellent control of that, he knew—but there may have been something new in his eyes that she was able to see.

For a moment Bessie's breath seemed to catch in her throat, and she blushed lightly.

She looked pleased, though. This handsome young man who was so favored by her father really was looking at her as a grown-up. Or soon to be a grown-up. It was a new and rather thrilling experience for her and one she had never known before.

Dwayne considered for a moment. They were alone in the church. Reverend Clawson would not return tonight, and no one else was likely to come either. The house was blocks away, and even if they didn't appear in time for supper, Mrs. Clawson was only likely to think that Bessie had gone with her father to help comfort the Turner family in their hour of loss.

The old bat had grandchildren, didn't she? Dwayne thought for a moment. He was almost sure that she did.

It was not inconceivable that the Reverend Clawson might have asked Bessie to come along and speak with them.

Not certain either, of course.

Bernard might come to remind them about supper.

Mrs. Clawson could even come herself to see if everything was all right.

Still, that would be small risk. Very small indeed.

And the grace that Dane was empowered to bestow took very little time.

Bessie flushed and dropped her eyes. She looked pleased by the attention he paid her but disconcerted, too. This was something she did not yet know how to handle.

Dwayne was conscious of the emptiness of the church. Of the gathering dusk beyond the windows.

He was conscious, too, though, of the opportunity that lay before him.

The studies the Reverend Clawson was directing him in were his chance to become a minister himself.

He would not be able to play the youth group member much longer. It was becoming more and more difficult to maintain a boyish, beardless appearance to the world.

Knowledge of Scripture and counsel was exactly what he needed if he wanted to continue his good works into the future.

And Bessie had time. She was not yet in the immediate danger of mortal sin. She was only now awakening to a knowledge of herself. Her sinful passions had not yet been stirred.

Dwayne laughed. "Elizabeth Clawson, you are blushing. Have I said something to . . . disturb you?"

She shook her head quickly. Too quickly. The faint blush became more vivid.

"Well, I certainly hope not. Are we friends?"

She nodded mutely. He could see, though, the quickening of her pulse at that tender, lovely hollow at her throat.

Dwayne chuckled. "I'm glad. I certainly want to be your friend."

"Me too." It came out as a half-throttled whisper.

Dwayne's smile now was truly gentle, truly affectionate.

He had time yet. But not much. Bessie was awakening to her fleshly nature. That was inevitable, of course. That was precisely what he was here to guard her against. But there was still time enough.

He could study under her father awhile longer before he granted her salvation from herself.

Abruptly, his decision made now, he turned and snapped closed the newly opened book her father had just given him. "I'll tell you what," he said in a cheery voice. "Just for tonight why don't I take a break from my studies. I'll walk you home and then, why, I'll volunteer to set the table tonight. If you promise me that afterward you shall play the piano for me."

She grinned.

"Four tunes of my choosing," he said. "Is it a deal?"

Bessie nodded eagerly.

"You won't try and wiggle out of it now, will you?"

"I promise," she said solemnly. Then with a giggle added, "Cross my heart I won't."

Her finger described a pair of quick cuts through the air immediately over those delicious little rosebuds, and Dwayne almost quivered at the wonderful new idea that had just come to him when she did that.

"Come along then," he said fondly. "We don't want to keep your mother waiting."

He offered his arm to her, and Bessie laid her fingertips on it shyly. No one had ever escorted her like *this* before, and it was as exciting as it was pleasurable.

If only some of the other girls could see her now. . . .

CHAPTER TWENTY-SEVEN

"Do you think he'll do it?"

Raider shrugged. "You want guarantees, Ted, see a snake oil salesman. I can't give you any."

"He acted like he would," Manton said. He was trying to convince himself, not Raider.

"Yup. An' maybe he will. Naw, I'd say it's stronger'n that. Prob'ly. Prob'ly he will." Raider grinned. "I hope."

Manton looked worried. But hopeful at the same time. Raider agreed. They were so *close*. At least potentially so close. If Dane Florette Sr. would go along with them, that is.

That was the thing. Would Florette come through on his promise and contact them the next time the boy communicated with his grandfather.

It was, really, their only hope to get a jump on the little son of a bitch. Otherwise they would be reduced to watching for news stories about dead girls and chasing along behind him.

Mopping up the blood left behind by a murderer was not Raider's idea of doing his job.

They needed to get ahead of Dane Florette for once. To nail the SOB and put a stop to him once and for all.

And for that they needed the assistance of Dane's own flesh and blood.

"Did you really mean what you told him?" Manton asked.

"About what?"

"About . . . you know . . . getting help for Fallon."

Raider found it odd that Manton persisted in referring to Florette as Fallon so often even though they were certain of Florette's real identity.

Or perhaps not so strange when he thought about it. It was a young man called Fallon who had murdered Ted Manton's little girl. It was Fallon Manton wanted to see brought down. Dane Florette was a crazy person who probably did need help. Fallon was an enemy to be hunted down and destroyed.

"It could happen like that," Raider said. "You never know what a court o' law will do. Judges can come up with the damnedest things sometimes. If the old man helps us and if we can find this Florette and put him in irons, and if a grand jury indicts him and if a trial jury convicts him, why, then a judge *might* rule that he oughta be put in an asylum instead of hung. You never know, Ted. Depends on the judge and on the defense lawyer."

"The grandfather would see to it that he has the best possible defense," Manton said. He looked worried.

"Ayuh. I think it's reasonable to believe that. The old man won't let the kid down. Hasn't that much use for him, but he's blood. The only blood kin old D.C. has left. He wouldn't let him swing if he could help it. If only because of how it would reflect on the family name, that old man couldn't allow it to happen. Better to let people think the kid slipped a cog than that he's a sonuvabitch pure and simple, I'd guess."

Manton frowned. "He could really go free?"

"No, damn it, I never said he could go free. I say he'll either swing on the gallows or be put in an insane asylum. Neither one of those is what I'd call free."

"Whatever happens, though, it all depends on D. C. Florette."

"More or less," Raider agreed. "Though we won't quit looking. We'll do our best. It's just that to be real honest with you, we don't have much chance to find him unless the old man comes through for us."

Manton grunted and lapsed into a sullenly introspective

silence on the sooty upholstery of the Union Pacific coach.

Raider stared out the window at the lush green foliage slipping past the speeding train.

Tomorrow, he thought. Tomorrow they would cross the Mississippi. He would feel better again after that. And better still when they crossed the Missouri into Nebraska.

Omaha would feel damned near like homecoming after Connecticut and New York and all those other overgrown, overpopulated, overbusy states that now were behind them.

Out where a man could see to the horizon and take a deep breath without choking on somebody else's floor sweepings was damn sure where Raider belonged. He was looking forward to getting back to it.

The arid, brown, high-desert hills of Nevada looked almighty good. Ted Manton, on the other hand, did not.

The butcher boy who had gotten on at the last whistle-stop made another pass through the coach, and Raider motioned for him to stop.

"Yes, sir?"

"Is that sandwich fresh?"

"You bet," the boy said with a grin that hinted it probably was not.

"I'll take it," Raider said. "And two apples. No, not that one. Those two in the corner. Got anything to drink in there?"

The boy shook his head and hooked a thumb toward the big steel pot at the front of the coach where stale water and a communal cup took care of thirst but not pleasure for the railroad passengers.

"These will do then," Raider said. He paid the outrageous fee the boy wanted for one sandwich and two apples, and the boy made his way back to the next coach in line.

The kid would get off at the next stop, load up his basket again, and ride the next eastbound passenger train back to his starting point, trying to peddle eatables to the folks on that train, too. It was a good job for a youngster, better than selling newspapers on a street corner. But the food sure wasn't much.

"Ted? Ted. Wake up, damn it." Raider had to shake the man by the shoulder to get his attention.

"What is it?"

"Here." Raider handed him the sandwich and one of the apples.

Manton shook his head. "I'm not hungry, thanks."

"Damn it, Ted, you haven't hardly eaten in two days." Or spoken either, Raider thought silently.

"I'm really not hungry, Raider."

Raider shook his head. But there wasn't much he could do about it short of taking the cheese sandwich and shoving it down the man's throat.

"I wish you'd eat."

"I couldn't. Really." Manton turned his head away and stared once again out the window. He had been doing little else since that conversation they had had back in... wherever the hell it had been. Indiana. Illinois. Someplace way the hell and gone behind them now.

Manton just sat and stared off into the distance with his eyes unfocused and his expression blank.

Raider was becoming worried about him.

Right now he looked as though if they accidentally wandered into a funeral parlor the mortician wouldn't even bother to call a doctor. Just get out his embalming fluids and go to work.

And Manton looked as if he wouldn't even care.

"You'll feel better if you—"

"Shut the fuck up," Manton snarled.

"Yeah. Sure." Raider gave up and took a bite out of the sandwich himself. It tasted like sawdust except that sawdust probably would have been more moist and pleasing to the palate. He tossed the rest of the awful thing out the window—Manton didn't even blink—and took a bite out of an apple. That was better.

"Are you sure I can't—"

Manton hunched his shoulders and turned in the seat so that his back was to Raider.

Raider sighed and gave up. By tomorrow night they would be in San Francisco. They could get a wire off to D. C. Florette from there to let the old man know where he could reach them.

Then, Raider realized, they damn sure better get busy looking for Dane the Third—make-work activity if nothing else—or Ted Manton was apt to curl up inside himself and just go ahead and die. He really looked that bad, Raider thought, and nothing Raider said or did or tried to do seemed to make any difference.

CHAPTER TWENTY-EIGHT

Fresno police chief Justin Carling greeted them with enthusiasm. The enthusiasm waned, though, when Raider admitted that they hadn't come for an arrest warrant.

"Actually, Chief, I was hoping you'd heard something," Raider admitted.

"Sorry," Carling said. "I got wires off to practically every lawman this side of New Orleans. The town council is already raising hell with me about the expense. But I haven't gotten anything back. No luck for you either?"

Raider filled the man in on their trip to Connecticut and what they had learned from D. C. Florette.

Carling had him go over the story about the father's death twice. "Do you know what it sounds like to me?" he asked when Raider was finally done.

Raider grinned at him. "Prob'ly the same thing I'd suspect. Though nobody will ever prove it."

Manton gave both men a curious look but said nothing. Which was entirely normal for him lately.

Carling, perhaps sensing Manton's depression, directed his comments to him and not Raider. "What I'd guess," the chief said, "is that this Dane Florette didn't find the house in flames. He came home that night and found his father in bed with that woman, killed the both of them, and set that fire himself. Think about it. He'd been torn apart first by his mother's screwing around, then by his grandfather's hard-nosed reactions, finally by his father being with another woman. It was too much for him. That right there, I'll bet, is where he lost touch with the real world."

"I take it one step further'n that," Raider mused.

"How so?"

"I'm thinking it might not have been some whore he found his father humping that night. I'm thinking it might have been Elizabeth Florette trying to come back for a Christmas reconciliation. It might've been his loved-hated mother that his father was bumping bellies with that night. Could've been both his parents he killed and set fire to."

"Son of a bitch," Carling muttered.

"Yeah. But we won't ever prove any of it. It's just guesswork."

"Won't make any difference anyway," Carling said. "If you can find Florette, he'll swing for the murder of Elizabeth O'Neill. After that it won't matter who else he might've killed. He'll be punished for all of them."

"That isn't what Raider told me," Manton spoke up.

"What do you mean?"

"Raider said there's always the chance Florette could get sent to an asylum instead of hanging. If old D.C. hires a smart enough lawyer to defend him."

Carling shrugged. "Not if I have anything to say about it."

"Can you guarantee me he'll hang?"

"Guarantee? Of course I can't guarantee it. Not in so many words. But I told you before . . ."

Manton stood and walked out of the office before Carling could finish.

"What's with him?" Carling asked.

"He's been like that practically ever since we left Connecticut. Won't eat. Won't talk. Mostly just sits and stares at nothing."

"It must be hard on him. The more he hears about the man who killed his little girl, the more he must have to brood about it. Rough."

"Yeah."

"You really think there's a chance the grandfather will tip you when he hears from the boy?"

"A chance, sure. But no guarantees."

"I'll tell you what I'd like to do, Raider. I'd like to swear you in as a special officer for this department and issue you a warrant for Florette's arrest. You know the sort. For Dane Florette III, a.k.a. Donald Flynn, a.k.a. John Doe. Just in case you aren't still in Fresno when you get a line on him."

Raider grinned. "You crafty son of a bitch," he said admiringly.

Carling grinned right back at him. "Damn right, mister. I want that boy brought back here to Fresno. Not no place else. Do you have a problem with that?"

Raider laughed. "No, Chief, I don't have any problem with that. It doesn't matter to me what jurisdiction he's tried under. Just so he comes to trial."

"You scratch my back and I'm sure as hell willing to scratch yours, mister Pinkerton man," the chief said.

"It's fair. I'll carry your warrant."

"You want the special officer's badge too?"

"I don't see why not."

"I'd prefer it, of course. It'd give me a better claim to the jurisdiction."

"Wait here. I have a tame J.P. upstairs who can swear you in and swear out the warrant at the same time. Just in case."

Carling excused himself and left the office. He had the legalistic paperwork accomplished within a half hour. Raider was impressed. Some lawmen couldn't seem to get anything done in less than a week. That was not a problem with Carling.

Raider returned to the cheap hotel room he was sharing with Manton, but there was no sign of the client.

Manton showed up late in the afternoon in time for dinner, and oddly enough, his depression seemed to have dissipated sometime during the afternoon.

He came in looking slightly sheepish but with an announcement that he was hungry as a bear and would Raider please hurry up so they could be there when the hotel restaurant began serving.

"Are you all right?" Raider asked.

"Yes. Now." He actually smiled. "Thanks for being so patient with me this past week."

"Sure. I'm just glad you're feeling better. Want me to fill you in on what me and the chief did after you left?"

"Of course. But couldn't we do that over supper? I swear I think I'm about to starve."

They went downstairs together, and Manton ordered more food for that one sitting than he had consumed during the entire past week.

Not only did he order it, he ate it. And was wanting desert when that was gone.

"What now?" Manton asked over coffee later.

"Pray, if you know how," Raider told him. "We need to hear from Florette or else get back some response to those wires Carling sent. I can't think of any other way to guess where the guy might be now."

Manton nodded and stirred some sugar into his coffee. Raider was pleased to see that he did not revert into his depression at all at the thought of the inactivity.

CHAPTER TWENTY-NINE

Reverend Clawson came in looking like the cat that ate the canary. Just a hint of a smile, and that more smug-looking than anything. Dwayne thought he looked like a man who was exceptionally pleased about something but who was trying not to show it.

"Yes, sir?"

Clawson was so pleased about whatever this was that he could not sit. He clasped his hands behind his back and paced up and down the length of the small office for a minute, savoring his enjoyment of the moment before breaking his news.

"Yes, uh, Dwayne." He tried not to smile, tried to look stern and forceful, but he couldn't bring it off.

"As you know, Dwayne, I've just come from a meeting with the Elders of the congregation."

"Yes, sir."

"I, uh, put forward a proposal for their consideration, Dwayne, I, uh . . . you will be happy to hear that they, uh, accepted my suggestion."

"Yes, sir?"

Clawson gave up his efforts to hide his enthusiasm and his face broke into a broad grin. "Dwayne, my boy, I am pleased to be able to tell you that this afternoon the Board of Elders issued an invitation for our congregation to have a guest speaker deliver the sermon Sunday morning next."

"Yes, sir?" Dwayne asked politely if without much real interest. "Who will we have the pleasure of hearing, sir?"

Clawson laughed. "You, Dwayne. *You* have been invited to deliver your first sermon this coming Sunday."

Dwayne was stunned. Genuinely taken completely aback. "But . . . I'm not qualified. I . . ."

Clawson chuckled and stepped forward to lay a hand affectionately on Dwayne's shoulder. "You are better prepared than you think, my boy. And I'll help you with it, of course. You *will* do it, won't you?"

"But . . . but I . . ." Dwayne too broke into a smile. "Yes," he declared firmly. "Yes, I will."

Clawson squeezed his arm and led him back to his desk. "Such a wonderful opportunity. Your very first sermon. Why, I daresay I'm as excited over this as I was when I delivered *my* first. Close your books now and get out pencil and paper. We have to begin working on your message."

Later, hours later, both Dwayne and the Reverend Clawson stepped away from their labors and stood to stretch wearily and walk about inside the confinement of the little office.

"I never knew it was so difficult," Dwayne said honestly. "You make it seem so easy each Sunday. I never realized how much hard work went into your preparations."

Clawson smiled. "But worthwhile, Dwayne. That's the thing. It is so very worthwhile. As you shall experience for yourself."

"Yes, sir."

"I have one word of warning to give you, though, lad. It is the message that is important. Not the clay vessel who delivers that message. After services Sunday you will walk with me down the aisle after I deliver the benediction. You will be there when the people leave. They will want to talk with you and shake your hand and tell you how fine your preaching was. Always remember, son, that it is the message that is truly important. Never the messenger. Never let worldly flattery turn your head, son. The temptations are there, and it is a delusion, a trap all too easy to fall into. Remember that and you will be fine. I know you will."

"I'll take your advice to heart, sir," Dwayne said seriously.

"I know you will." He smiled again. "Son."

Dwayne grinned back at him. "While we're taking a break, sir, could we walk down to the soda parlor for an iced ade? My treat, sir."

"Why, that would be nice, Dwayne. Thank you."

They retrieved their coats from the rack and left the cool interior of the church for the dry warmth of the afternoon sunlight.

"I've been thinking, sir," Dwayne mused aloud as they walked, making it up as he went along, "and it has been bothering me for some time that the church needs new hymnals. The old ones are awfully tattered."

"True enough that we could use new ones, but frankly, Dwayne, we can't afford them. The freight charges alone are more than we could pay, much less the cost of initial purchase. For as many as we would need . . ."

"I am quite capable of making the donation, sir. If you would permit it, that is."

"Dwayne, I didn't . . . I mean I never . . ."

Dwayne Forbes laughed with true pleasure. He could scarcely remember when he had felt so pleased about anything before. All the opportunities that lay before him now. His studies. The sermon—the acid test of whether he was ready to assume a youth ministry role on his own, without Clawson there to guide him—and of course sweet Bessie, who would soon be saved from her own sinful nature. Everything. Just everything was wonderful.

He wanted to make some outward gesture to express his delight.

"I've seen you admiring the literature on the new *Compleat Hymnal and Book of Praise,* sir. Why don't I just order some of those shipped? Say, four hundred copies?"

"Oh, I couldn't let you do that, lad. That is an expensive work. And with the shipping costs, it would be . . . more than a thousand dollars, I should say. Nearer two."

Dwayne felt so fine that he threw his head back and

practically shouted his joy. "Wonderful! We'll consider it settled. It will be my gift and my pleasure. And believe me, sir, I can easily afford it."

"I—I couldn't," Clawson stammered, although the eager pleasure in his expression showed that he could.

At the soda parlor Dwayne secured a pair of iced lime-ades and they carried them outside to the umbrellaed shade of a tiny wrought-iron table. Now that Clawson had accepted the idea of the new hymnals he was full of enthusiasm for using them. Their talk was interrupted by the passage of two men on the sidewalk. The two were several paces beyond the table when they stopped and one of them turned back.

"Bernie," he said to Clawson, extending a hand. "I was so busy I almost didn't notice you here." He gave Dwayne a smile and a handshake too. "Would this be the young man you were telling me about?"

"Indeed he is, Charles. Dwayne Forbes, Charles Moore. Dwayne has accepted our invitation, Charles. He'll speak on Sunday. Try not to miss it this time."

Moore grinned and shrugged. "You know how it is, Bernie. Saturday night and Sunday morning are our busiest times. Bring them in on Saturday night and process them out on Sunday morning."

"Charles is our sheriff," Clawson explained for Dwayne's benefit. "He is also a member of our Board of Elders, but ever since he was appointed sheriff he's been too busy to attend services as regularly as he used to."

"Another few months, Bernie. Then we'll have a properly elected sheriff and I can be just another citizen again." To Dwayne he added, "I'm only filling in the balance of old Sheriff Kunstler's term."

"Won't you join us, Charles?"

"No time I'm afraid. But I'll try to make it to hear this young gentleman's sermon on Sunday." He winked at Clawson. "Now I see what you meant, Bernie. Sorry I ever brought it up."

"No harm done, Charles."

"Of course not. Well then, gentlemen. If you will excuse me?" Moore touched the brim of his derby and rejoined his companion, who was waiting impatiently some steps away.

"What was that last comment about?" Dwayne asked after they resumed their seats.

"What do you mea . . . oh, that. About no harm having been done?"

Dwayne nodded.

Clawson chuckled. "When we were discussing you at our board meeting, Charles mentioned a telegram he received recently. Something about a desperate type of person who goes around the countryside committing murders. A rather nice-looking young man, apparently, who invariably uses the initials D. and F. in his assumed names. Charles's curiosity was aroused when I spoke about you, but of course I assured him there was no possible connection. My goodness, lad, I know you better than *that*, don't I?" Clawson laughed.

Dwayne laughed too, but he had to force it. The sound of it was hollow to him, though, and he could feel a rising pressure behind his ears, a force like the clutch of a tight fist around his suddenly racing heart.

It took all his powers of concentration to insure that he showed nothing of what he was feeling to his table companion.

A telegraphic message. A warning. A murderer. (Would they *never* learn to understand that he was saving these young women, *not* harming them?) A young man. The initials D. and F.

That was a mistake!

Why oh why hadn't he seen that before? Why hadn't he realized it? Especially now that all his monogrammed luggage and clothing were lost. It was no longer really necessary to cling to those initials. How could he have been so blind to the dangers?

"Dwayne?"

Dwayne Forbes blinked and realized that Reverend

Clawson was touching his wrist, shaking him slightly. The preacher had been saying something and Dwayne had not noticed, so far lost was he in the concerns of the unexpected.

"Oh. Uh." He smiled. "I'm sorry. I was thinking about my . . . our . . . sermon. The next passage." The smile became easier. "Sorry. What were you saying, sir?"

Clawson had looked worried for a moment. Now the older man relaxed. "Perfectly understandable, son. I daresay I was hopeless the entire week before my first appearance at the pulpit. What I was saying was that we should stop by the market on our way back to the church. I think the news of the day calls for a celebration at dinner tonight. Something special, eh?"

Dwayne smiled, his composure fully recovered now. "Yes, sir, I think that would be a wonderful idea. Roast duckling, perhaps, with oyster dressing? It would be my pleasure to have the butcher shop send the ingredients to the house. If you don't think it would be too much of an imposition on Mrs. Clawson."

Clawson squeezed his forearm. "You are always so considerate, lad. No imposition. I'll see to it."

"And I'll arrange for the ducks and oysters to be delivered," Dwayne said.

"We have a great deal to celebrate tonight."

"Yes, sir. Indeed we do."

Dwayne smiled. But inwardly his stomach continued to churn sourly at the narrowness of his escape from Sheriff Charles Moore.

He had made a mistake, he acknowledged silently to himself. It was an error he would never repeat.

CHAPTER THIRTY

Dwayne let himself into his room. The hotel staff—efficient if expensive—had been there before him. A lamp with a low-trimmed wick was burning on the bedside table, and the bed was already turned back ready for him even though he was back hours earlier than usual.

He had excused himself from the Clawson home almost immediately after dinner, without the normal ritual of studying in Reverend Clawson's library. The family undoubtedly attributed the early departure to excitement.

In fact, it was worry.

He could not stop thinking about what Reverend Clawson had said that afternoon.

A telegraph message to the sheriff. And if to the sheriff here then presumably to law enforcement agencies throughout California. Perhaps even further, beyond the borders of this state into others.

Someone—in Olympia, perhaps, or Fresno—was looking for a young man, a killer, with the initials D. and F.

Dwayne—Dane—was no longer in shock, but he certainly was concerned.

He had to plan. He had to avoid mistakes in the future.

Avoid mistakes? He hadn't realized he was *making* mistakes.

That was the truly frightening thing about it, now that he had the time and the privacy to consider.

From now on he was going to have to exercise extreme care. In everything. From his choice of names onward.

He removed his suit coat and hung it carefully on a wooden hanger in the wardrobe, removed his tie and collar, and put on a light smoking jacket. He needed to twease his neck and chin for new hairs, but first he wanted to think.

He almost wished he had a drink right now. A stout one, even though he usually abhorred strong spirits.

Barring that he opened the French doors to the balcony, letting a salt-scented breeze fill his suite, and went outside to sit in the darkness with the cool ocean air laving him.

The sea was a vast, dark expanse lying for unimaginable distances to the west. A last-quarter sliver of moon and a light layer of scattered cloud gave nothing but hints of the immense bulk of the ocean and of the restlessness of its waves.

Dwayne was beginning to feel a similar restlessness within himself.

Perhaps, he thought, he should abandon everything here. Just get up, pack, and walk out *right now.*

Except he was doing so *well* here.

Everything was going so wonderfully right here.

His studies. His preparations for ordainment—even if, admittedly, it would be a self-ordainment, still it would be a thoroughly convincing one once he was done here. The immeasurably valuable experience he would gain this week in the preparation of a sermon and on Sunday in the actual delivery before a real congregation. That in itself was a priceless experience that would be impossible to duplicate in any other way.

And of course, perhaps best of all, there was Bessie. Elizabeth. She needed him.

Without even knowing it, she needed him.

She was nearing the age of dangerous lustfulness, even though neither she nor anyone else seemed aware of that quite yet.

Tonight at dinner she had made a point of serving him the plumpest pieces of duckling and the most moist and oyster-filled portion of the oven-baked dressing.

Her parents, if they noticed at all, undoubtedly thought

the child had an innocent crush on their frequent house-guest.

Dwayne knew better.

The way Elizabeth looked at him now. The way the heartbeat visible at her throat quickened when he was near. The way her fingertips had brushed past the back of his neck when she bent to refill his water glass.

Those were all signs of her sinful nature coming to the fore.

For his own sake, Dwayne Forbes should probably pack and leave this place immediately.

For Elizabeth's he dared not. He had to remain long enough to save her from herself.

He had to show her the horrors of lust and anoint her in the blood of salvation.

It was his duty. His mission. And no one but he could grant her this eternal comfort.

The breeze freshened, and Dwayne shivered.

No! He would not leave. Not yet. Not quite yet.

First the sermon.

Then Elizabeth.

Then—mercifully—he would be free to leave.

But never again, he told himself, would he be so unwise as to cling to those old initials.

From now on . . . He mulled the ideas slowly. No longer quite so afraid of discovery. Able to savor his plans once again, for the first time since that rude shock of the afternoon when the sheriff chanced by.

He had come west for safety after saving those girls in the Northeast. Now, it seemed, the West too was becoming dangerous for him. Men were looking for him here.

There was always Canada. But he would be a foreigner there. He would stand out too readily from the crowd. And it was the camouflage of innocent participation that made him so successful.

Perhaps instead he should journey next to the South.

Southern girls . . . he shivered again, but this time there was no breeze.

Southern girls were particularly wicked. Or so he had heard.

There was that Southern boy at the horrid school where the old bastard exiled Dane Florette.

The boy had been a braggart and a liar and Dane had despised him, but he had talked much about Southern girls, and he would not have been lying about that.

Southern girls valued their virginity—if only because Southern men demanded virginity in their brides—but the Southern girls were hot-blooded and lustful. That was what that boy had said. What was his name? Dwayne couldn't remember. Not that it mattered. What mattered was what the boy had said about Southern girls, even about his own sisters.

He had claimed that Southern girls absolutely refused to give up their virginity but that they were passionate. Even demanding. When tongue-kissed, he said, they refused to go all the way with a boy, but they would use their mouths on practically any man.

Southern girls were well known for sucking cock.

Wantonly. Immorally. Frequently.

They preserved the appearance of honor by remaining virgins, but they willingly took hard cocks into their mouths and sucked until the juices flowed, and delighted in swallowing the seed that was so produced.

Dwayne shuddered again and felt himself grow hard at the thought of spurting his juices into a Southern girl's hot, eager mouth.

That was lust. That was sin. That was every bit as foul and evil as fucking.

That, too, he could save them from.

Elizabeth was there in the South. He was sure that she was. He could save her from herself when he found her there.

He pulled open the front of his smoking jacket and touched himself through the broadcloth of his trousers.

The bulge behind his fly was insistent now.

Elizabeth!

There was no light on the balcony. No one could see. There was nothing before him but the broad, empty sweep of the ocean.

He slowly unfastened the buttons that confined him and reached for a clean handkerchief into which he could spend his seed.

Elizabeth!

She needed him.

He would find her in the South, and she would want to take him into her mouth. But she was here, too, in beautiful California.

She would be sleeping now, not two dozen blocks away, in the upstairs of the Clawson home.

Dwayne had had occasion once to go upstairs looking for young Bernard. He had paused at Elizabeth's open door and looked into her bedroom when the rest of the family was downstairs in the parlor.

It was a childish room, decorated in flounces and ruffles and rag-stuffed toys. That was a deception. A delusion. Dwayne knew what her true nature was. He could sense it whenever he looked at her, and he was determined to save her.

He could visualize her this minute. Sleeping. Curled on her side, her hair loosened to fan softly over her pillow.

Moonlight streaming through her open window to outline the curve of her cheeks, the seemingly innocent bow of her lips, the tenderness of her throat.

His breathing came more heavily, and he began to stroke himself lightly. Very lightly. Very slowly now.

Elizabeth!

He had never saved a girl so young. Her body was only now beginning to form. The seeds of wickedness were already there in her heart, of course, but her body was still so small and so tender.

She would be tight. He knew that. She would be exceptionally tight. It would hurt him to penetrate her. And when he did she would writhe and cry out from the pain of it—

the cleansing pain of it—and would try to move away from him.

He would have to hold her down. He would have to ram himself into her with force.

Probably, like the Elizabeth he had saved in Fresno, he should take the precaution of moistening himself in her mouth before he entered. In her fear she would be dry.

Not like that one in Providence or Beth in Wilmington. They had been almost beyond salvation. They protested, yes, but when he entered them their lustful bodies betrayed them and they became moist and quiescent at his entry. There was no pain with them. He did not even think Beth had been a virgin, although she protested that she was. Lying bitch. Cunt!

They were all cunts, of course.

He knew that. He proved it. And in spite of that he saved them.

His hand was moving faster now, squeezing harder, and he thought once again of the Elizabeth here, of Bessie who was asleep in her bedroom in seeming innocence.

Her dreams were vile, he knew.

Her dreams were filled with the sweaty, sinful coupling of male and female bodies.

Dwayne would cure her of that. It was his gift to be able to do so. And—he smiled—Bessie's father was helping to make it possible for him to continue on into the future without end.

Future without end. It was a good phrase. He might have to put that into his notes for the sermon. Future without end.

Elizabeth. Bessie.

He could practically see her now. He could visualize her. Naked. Slim. Faint swell of hip. Tiny, rose-tipped bud of breast. Slender, delicate column of throat.

Did she have hair yet?

Dwayne smiled.

Soon, very soon, he would know.

He visualized her both ways. With a thin patch of

lightly curling hair. Nude and baldly unprotected there.

He hadn't yet actually *seen* a hairless cunt. He could imagine it.

His hand moved faster and harder against his shaft, and the excitement in him built. With his other hand he cupped the wadded handkerchief over himself.

He would take his time with Bessie. It would be easy enough to arrange. She trusted him. The whole family trusted him. She might even betray her true nature by *joining* him in her newfound lust.

Certainly he would take his time with Bessie and strip her naked and spread her legs wide and . . .

He groaned and stiffened, and hot fluids poured out of him into the receptacle of the cloth.

Soon enough that seed would be spent in a receptacle of hot, bleeding flesh.

He stiffened for a moment and then went limp, utterly exhausted. He might even have passed out for a moment.

When he recovered he buttoned his trousers and pulled his smoking jacket back into place and stood, enjoying the feel and the smell of the breeze coming off the dark ocean.

First he had to finish his preparations for the future. And send off the order for those books. He wondered if he had enough cash remaining to do that first thing in the morning. Probably. But he would need more very soon. Enough to take him in comfort and style to the South.

He was needed in the South.

He knew that now.

Elizabeth was in the South. She needed him. She was waiting for him there. As quickly as he was done here, he would go and find her.

Relaxed and smiling now, Dwayne Forbes went inside and went to bed. His thoughts as he floated gently into sleep were of the limitless, wondrous opportunities that lay in his future.

CHAPTER THIRTY-ONE

Raider scowled unhappily at the big bowl in the center of the long communal table. A waiter was coming out of the kitchen, but he was only bringing more of the same gray shit. Raider knew it, and he resented it.

Sure enough, the waiter, a greasy, ugly man wearing an apron that was about as greasy as his hair was, upended a huge pot over the nearly empty bowl and another glop of thick, lumpy oatmeal dropped wetly into the bowl.

Raider was heartily sick of the way he was having to eat with Manton running low on funds. Oatmeal or cornmeal mush for breakfast. Fried mush or maybe boiled potatoes for lunch. Boiled meat and cabbage for supper. Raider was sick of it.

Still, he didn't complain. Manton was about at the end of his rope and had no choice. And *he* certainly wasn't complaining. If anything, for the past couple of days he had been acting and sounding and looking better than he had since Raider first met him. Raider didn't want to rock the boat for the poor soul, so he kept his mouth shut and reached for the bowl of oatmeal.

The other men already at the cheap table were wolfing down their huge portions of the awful stuff as if they actually liked it. Raider found that a bit difficult to understand. Breakfast should be ham and eggs or chops and spuds or sausage and flannel cakes or ... or almost anything but this. The other men, dressed as laborers or worse, did not seem to mind it at all. Possibly they were just glad to be getting something to eat. There was likely something in

that after all. Raider smiled at Manton and dropped a lad-
leful of the bland oatmeal into his bowl. He pushed the
bowl toward Manton.

"Thanks, I . . ."

There was a pause in the activity of the other men at the
table, many of them looking toward the door, several
quickly diverting their eyes away from the door and
coughing into their fists or wiping dry lips. Activity at the
table ceased as suddenly as if a valve had been clamped
shut over it.

Raider looked up and saw with some amusement that it
was only a police officer who had come in, a young man
wearing the blue coat and cap of Chief Carling's department.

The young copper looked around and spotted Raider and
Manton. He hurried toward them, ignoring the other men
—probably, Raider realized, to those fellows' great relief
—and touched the brim of his uniform cap.

"The chief sent me t' find you," the cop said in a quick
rush of breath. "You're to come on the double-quick an'
meet him at the Western Union office. Wire comin' in, sir.
He said for me to find you an'—"

Raider was already on his feet, Manton beside him.

"Is it . . . ?" Manton began.

"Don't know, sir. The chief said to find you and fetch
you. The message wasn't all received when we got word."

"It has to be," Raider said.

They hurried outside, the cop coming right behind
them.

Two blocks down the street, Chief Carling and a Western Union messenger were heading toward them at a fast
walk that was almost a jog. The chief broke into an awkward, loping run when he saw them. Even before he was
within speaking distance he was calling out to them.

"It's come. The wire from Connecticut. It's here."

For the sake of propriety it was the Western Union employee who was waving the yellow message form ad-

dressed to Raider, but it was the Fresno police chief who was grinning and doing the talking.

"This is it," he said as the two parties finally came together in the middle of the business district.

The messenger handed the form to Raider, and he turned it so that Ted Manton could read it also.

> REQUEST FOR FUNDS RECEIVED THIS AYEM STOP POINT OF ORIGIN REDONDO COMMA CALIFORNIA STOP WILL RESPOND AS AGREED STOP INFORM ME IMMEDIATELY AS TO OUTCOME STOP HAVE ALREADY NOTIFIED MY ATTORNEY STOP REMEMBER YOUR PROMISES STOP

It was signed D. C. Florette Sr.

"What promises?" Carling demanded.

Raider was busy rereading the message. He glanced up at Carling with annoyance and asked a question of his own, "Where the hell is Redondo?"

"South. Down along the coast. Now what's this about promises? That son of a bitch is to be tried in my jurisdiction, by God, or I'll—"

"He'll be tried here," Raider assured him. "I'll go wrap him up and bring him back here. I only told the old man I'd take him alive and unharmed if there's any human way to do that and that he'll get a fair trial and a good lawyer. That's all I promised."

"And this agreement he mentions right here?" Carling pointed to the text of the telegram.

"He said when he heard from the boy he'd wait two days to give us time to get to the Western Union office ahead of the bank draft. We'll be there waiting when Dane Florette calls for his money. Snap the cuffs on him there, and that'll be that."

Carling nodded.

"We can get to Redondo inside of two days?"

"Easy," Carling assured him. "We can."

"We?"

"The three of us. I'm going too."

Raider shrugged. "Doesn't matter to me. Just so long as he wouldn't recognize you from when he was here and murdered the O'Neill girl."

Carling shook his head. "No chance of that that I know of."

"All right, then. How do we get to Redondo?"

"There's a train leaving in a few hours. I'll meet you at the station. You can be packed in time, I take it?"

"Chief, we'd leave without bags before we let Florette slip away from us now."

"Good. I'll see you in an hour. At the depot."

"We'll be there," Raider assured him.

CHAPTER THIRTY-TWO

"I don't believe this," Raider fumed. "I don't fucking believe it." A man at the front of the passenger coach who was traveling with a smartly dressed woman turned to glare at Raider's language, then flushed and pretended disinterest after he saw the answering look Raider gave him.

"Conductor! Damn it, man, I demand that you do something about this," Carling barked at the harried-looking railroad employee who was delivering the bad news to the Southern Pacific passengers. "I demand you do something at once."

Of the three of them it was, oddly, only Ted Manton who seemed to be taking the delay calmly.

The conductor had just informed them that southbound service had been disrupted by a damaged bridge.

"I'm terribly sorry, gentlemen, but there is nothing more I can do. We already have repair crews out working. They haven't reported back yet how long it will take to rebuild the bridge."

"They have to rebuild the whole damn thing?"

"There was a flash flood, sir. I'm sorry. The bridge washed out, and there is simply nothing we can do about it. We can't run without rails, after all." The conductor did his best to seem polite, but he was obviously not in a mood to listen to passenger complaints when he had better things to do.

"At least they stopped us at a town and not out in the middle of nowhere," Manton said. "Couldn't we go on somehow? Find an alternate form of transportation and press on? It could be days before they get a bridge reconstructed."

Raider was still upset, but he wasn't going to be stupid about it. "Yeah, damn it, that's about all we can do. But it'll be slower. There's no guarantee we can get to the telegraph office in time to grab Florette there now."

"That's easily taken care of," Manton said calmly. "We'll simply wire old Mr. Florette to delay sending the bank draft until he hears from us. Then it hardly matters if we are later than we expected."

Carling nodded. "That makes sense."

"Yeah. Okay. Let's get our bags and see where we can hire a coach. You two take care of that. I'll get the wire off to Florette."

They left the stalled train and went back to the baggage car to collect their gear. The remainder of this trip might not be so easy as the first part had been.

CHAPTER THIRTY-THREE

"You paid it? You've already fucking paid it?" Raider
roared.

"How could you've paid it? I sent a wire just yesterday
telling the old man to delay sending it!" Raider's fist
crashed down on the counter, and the Western Union operator flinched.

"I . . . I'm sorry, sir," he stammered. "I wouldn't know
anything about that, of course. Although there were some
telegraph lines that went down north of here when a bridge
washed out. If the operator there normally used a southern
routing, your wire might have been delayed until—"

"I don't care about that, damn it. You're telling us you
already got that draft authorization in and already paid it
out to D. C. Florette III?"

"Yes, sir. As I already told you, sir. The draft came in
early this afternoon. The young gentleman called for it not
more than two hours ago. Just before closing time for the
banks, sir. He signed for receipt of the draft. See?" The
man picked up a ledger, opened it to a page toward the
back, and showed it to them. Carling groaned. The signature of their man was there.

Florette Senior somehow had failed to receive Raider's
wire in time. The bank draft had been sent, exactly as they
agreed, after exactly the delay Raider had asked for. But
too soon. The arrest party hadn't been there in time to
capture Florette III at the telegraph office.

"Jesus," Raider groaned.

"We'll find him," Carling said. "He's still in town. He

174

hasn't completed his plans here or we would have heard. We can start looking in the churches. That's his pattern, right? We can canvass every church in this area until we find him."

"Couldn't we ask the local law officials for help?" Manton suggested. "They would have more manpower than the three of us can offer."

"Good idea, Ted. We'll get cracking on it. Check every church congregation from San Diego to Santa Barbara if we have to. He has to be at one of them, and we know he'll have the same initials. There can't be too many new-comers like that. We'll find him."

Raider looked at the Western Union clerk, who acted ready to bolt if this tall stranger barked at him again. "Where can we find your local law?"

The man swallowed uncomfortably. "The courthouse is two blocks down on the square. The sheriff's office is on the second floor."

"Two blocks?"

"Yes, sir. Right down that way."

"Let's go," Raider said. He needn't have bothered. Chief Carling and Ted Manton were already halfway to the door, and he had to hurry to catch up with them.

"Are you sure of what you're saying?" Sheriff Charles Moore demanded.

"Absolutely," Carling told him. "The man is wanted for murder in Fresno and on multiple counts of other murders elsewhere as well. The Pinkerton operative here and this gentleman have been on his trail for quite some time. I have a warrant for his arrest here." He produced the document and handed it to Moore. "Will you assign us some men to help with the search?"

Moore puffed out his cheeks, paused for a moment, and then exhaled very slowly. "No need for that."

"Come again?"

"I said there isn't any need to conduct a search. I already know where your man is. He . . . the son of a bitch

delivered the sermon in my own church just yesterday
morning. I've met him myself. He seems—"

"—charming," Raider finished for him. "The complete
and perfect young gentlemen. It's how he cozens his victims. Although we don't fully understand why. Unfortunately, Sheriff, we have all too much experience with how
he does it."

Moore looked quite thoroughly miserable. "There
couldn't possibly be any mistake?"

"Absolutely no chance of it," Carling declared.

"Then let's go find him. I don't know where he lives,
but we can check with Bernie Clawson. Bernie is our pastor, you understand. This Forbes fellow's mentor, so to
speak. Bernie will know where we can find him."

"Forbes? And a first name beginning with a D, of
course."

"Dwayne," Moore said. "Dwayne Forbes. He seems so
. . . likable."

"Sure. Except for that one little flaw."

The four of them left the courthouse. It was late, and
they were lucky to have caught the sheriff at his office. He
had been working late, conferring with the county supervi-
sors about the approaching election campaign, or they
might not have found him at all that evening. Fortunately,
Charles Moore preferred politics to food any day of the
week.

"It isn't far," Moore said when they reached the street.
"It'll be quicker to walk than look for a cab."

The four of them set out at a brisk walk with Moore in
the lead. It occurred to Raider that of all of them, he
seemed to be the only one who was armed in anticipation
of this arrest. Neither the Redondo sheriff nor the Fresno
police chief was openly carrying a weapon, anyway.

With luck, though, it would not be that kind of arrest.

A man whose bent is the rape and knifing of innocent
young women would not likely have the stomach to face a
grown man. Probably Florette would submit without problem once they confronted him, that situation with Sheriff

Simmons in Washington State notwithstanding. Florette was a bastard, but he certainly wasn't stupid. He had proved that well enough in the past.

"Right in this next block," Moore said, increasing his stride.

CHAPTER THIRTY-FOUR

Dwayne could not remember ever being happier.

The sermon yesterday had been a success. More than a success. It had been thrilling. Standing in front of all those people and delivering a message to them. All their attention focused on him and on him alone. And then afterward the handshakes and the extravagance of their praise.

It had been a heady experience indeed. He could understand now the admonition Reverend Clawson gave him to beware a sense of personal power, even grandeur, afterward. It would be a trap all too easy to fall into. He would have to be wary of it in the future.

Dwayne grinned, conscious of all the marvelous opportunities that lay before him in that unseen but no doubt delightful future.

Bessie, walking beside him, saw the expression and apparently misunderstood it. She was walking with her fingertips quite properly on his arm. She gave him a little squeeze. "Thanks for asking me to come with you this evening."

Dane smiled down at her. "It's my pleasure, Elizabeth. Truly."

The girl blushed slightly, but he could see that she was pleased. Her little brother had wanted to come along—Dwayne had said something about preparing a nice surprise—and she had practically taken his head off to keep him from spoiling her walk with Dwayne. He hadn't had to say a word about it.

It was only more proof, of course, of the wrongful nature that was building in her. He was going to be able to reach her with salvation just barely in time.

That thought too pleased him, and he smiled down at her with love and joy in his heart for her, for her family, for everyone.

Nearly everything he needed to do here was accomplished.

He had learned quite enough by now to successfully launch a youth ministry. And all his obligations here had been met. The new hymnals were ordered and paid for in advance. He had taken care of that this afternoon, and he and Reverend Clawson had dropped the order in the mail on their way home for an early supper.

Now there was only Elizabeth's salvation to see to here, and he could be gone.

There was a coach leaving at nine. He already had his ticket to be on it.

Dane snickered softly to himself. Not that he would be on it. He needed very little. He had learned that in the past few months. In a way that unpleasantness up in Washington had been a blessing to him. It showed him how little he really needed in the way of worldly possessions. Anything he needed he could buy wherever he was. His money belt was full. He could walk away from here. When they looked for him they would trace the route of the night coach. Instead he would walk up the beach and take a boat south. Make a landing somewhere in the vicinity of San Diego and outfit himself anew for the trip east to . . . he thought about that again while he walked. Probably to New Orleans to begin with. Then on to . . . He grinned. There was a whole world out there waiting for him. Mississippi. Alabama. Georgia. Elizabeth was waiting for him there, and she needed him.

And in the meantime . . .

He smiled down at Elizabeth.

They reached the walkway to her father's church and turned onto it.

He had told the family that he and Bessie would be

working on a surprise—well, it would be—and that they might be late, for them not to worry. He had her parents' permission to keep her out late tonight. No one would think to look for them until Dane was long, long gone and Elizabeth was safe from all temptation and sin.

It could not have been any more perfect.

"You still haven't told me what the surprise is, Dwayne," Bessie said as he led her into the sanctuary and over toward the stairs that went up to the choir loft.

Dane blinked, forgetting for a moment that he was still Dwayne. In his thoughts he had already gone ahead to being someone else. But not with the telltale initials this time. George, he thought. He had always liked the name George. George, um, Forrest? No, no F this time. George Smith? Too common. George Smythe. That was better.

But for now, for the next little while, he was still Dwayne Forbes to Bessie. Soon enough, of course, Elizabeth would recognize him as Dane.

And when that was done, he would once again set Dane aside until he was needed.

Dane quivered with delight at the joy of it all and led Bessie up the narrow stairs.

"Have you been hiding something up here, Dwayne?"

"You'll see," he promised. "Just another few minutes and you'll see."

She smiled at him and squeezed his arm again, pleased and flattered that this handsome, fine young gentleman was taking such a grown-up interest in her.

He led her to the topmost pew in the loft and sat close beside her.

"There's something I'd like to do before I show you the surprise, Elizabeth."

Bessie nodded, her eyes wide with nervousness and her heart racing with anticipation. She could almost believe that Dwayne actually wanted to *kiss* her, impossible though that might seem.

There was that liquid softness in his eyes and—it was not the sort of thing she was supposed to notice, but she was almost certain too that there was that funny bulge in his trousers that boys got sometimes, although she had *never* seen a grown man do that before. But then no grown man had ever looked at her the way Dwayne was right now.

One thing she knew for sure, and that was that Dwayne would never do anything to hurt her or that was wrong. Her dad and her mom had both told her that, and they would know.

Dwayne leaned nearer, his face looming close over hers, so close that she could feel his breath warm against her mouth. She closed her eyes, her lips parting slightly and her heart a wildly beating lump in her throat. She had never been kissed before. Not even by a boy. And Dwayne . . .

Dane's arm slipped behind Bessie's shoulders, and he pressed his lips gently to hers.

She was trembling slightly. He could feel the tiny tremors race through her body and her lips. Her kiss was soft and tentative. She tasted lightly of mint. He remembered that she had had a glass of cold minted tea before they left the house.

Very slowly, very shyly, Bessie's arms crept up to encircle his neck, and her lips parted as she returned his kiss.

Dane could feel the rising pressure in his loins. But he was in no hurry here. He had planned everything carefully. He had time.

He kissed her again, her response quicker and more eager this time, and Bessie moaned a little at the giddiness his touch caused in her.

Dane's tongue probed outward, seeking entry to her mouth.

Bessie stiffened and her eyes popped wide in shock.

Kissing was one thing, but . . .

Dane laughed happily.

Elizabeth was there, hiding just under the surface of innocent Bessie. Just as he knew she was.

The bitch.

The whore.

The Jezebel.

He tightened his grip around her shoulders, and his free hand pressed rough and hard against her chest.

She tried to struggle away from him, but he was much too strong for her.

Her mouth opened, this time with no thought of tenderness or kissing, and he covered it quickly, roughly with his own. Drinking in the taste of her newfound fear. Sucking into himself her warm, moist breath.

She wrenched herself from side to side, trying now to escape. Dane pulled and twisted, forcing her down onto the pew beneath him until he was lying half on top of her, one strong leg pinning her body under his while he groped and clawed and pulled at her flesh.

Her clothes. That damned dress. He had to get it off of her. He had to expose her fully for the whore that she was.

He tugged and ripped, pulling and tearing in a frenzy now.

Bessie tried to scream, and he clamped a palm over the bitch Elizabeth's opened mouth.

Now. Now! Dane exulted silently. *NOW!*

CHAPTER THIRTY-FIVE

The men charged through the unlocked front door of the church, Raider in the lead with his Remington in his fist, Moore and Carling and Manton close behind, a puffing and winded Bernie Clawson trailing by some yards.

There was no sign of Bessie and Florette. The door to Clawson's office stood open, the small room empty.

"Wh—"

Raider held a finger to his lips. "Shhh."

Faint sounds reached him. A muffled cry. The thump of something hard—a shoe? a fist?—against wood.

"Upstairs," Raider said.

Clawson, just gaining the doorway, pointed toward the staircase that was hidden in the shadows at the side of the foyer, and Raider bounded toward it with the others on his heels.

He took the steps three at a time and burst into the loft with his revolver leveled.

The bastard was there! And so was the little girl.

Florette was struggling with Bessie, pinning her down with his body and pawing and grasping at her, trying to rip her clothing away.

He seemed totally unaware that he was no longer alone in the choir loft with his intended victim.

Raider couldn't shoot. There was too much chance of hitting the girl.

He hesitated for a moment, and Carling bumped into him from the force of the angry chief's charge. Then both of them recovered and raced up to the topmost pew.

Carling's fist descended in a hammering blow onto the back of Florette's neck, and Raider could hear Florette's teeth jolt together at the impact of the unexpected blow.

The Fresno police chief grabbed Florette by the scruff of the neck and literally hauled him off the terrified girl, holding him up at arm's length in an incredible display of raw strength.

Carling punched Florette in the belly, slammed him into the next pew, and began hitting him in the face.

Raider and the others attended to the sobbing, nearly hysterical little girl. Her father wrapped his arms tight around her and turned her head away from the sight of Justin Carling beating Dane Florette.

"Easy now, Chief," Moore said. "Easy."

Carling ignored him, continuing to rain punches onto Dane Florette's unprotected face and head. Florette seemed to be in too deep a state of shock to understand what was happening. He made no effort to defend himself.

"Raider," Moore said.

Raider nodded and stepped forward. Between them, he and Moore were able to grab Carling's arms and stop the man's flailing.

"It's all right now," Moore said soothingly. "We have him. You can stop now. It's over."

Carling was shaking from the extent of his emotions. His teeth were chattering like a man in the last extremes of cold, and his knees were wobbly.

Gradually he brought himself under control and was able to gasp for breath.

"Do you want to put the cuffs on him?" Moore offered.

Carling nodded toward Raider. "That pleasure belongs to Raider, I think."

Florette continued to sit where Carling had dropped him, slumped in the corner of the pew. He was bleeding from the nose and the mouth and from a number of cuts that had been opened on his cheeks and over his eyes. When those bruises began to puff and color he probably would be unrecognizable for weeks to come, Raider guessed.

Raider pulled out his set of handcuffs and stepped forward. Then a thought struck him and he turned to Ted Manton, who was hanging back watching.

"Ted, it's been a long road here. Do you want to do it?"

Raider expected agreement. Pleasure. Relief. Something.

Instead Ted Manton stared blankly at the man who had murdered his only daughter those long, terrible months before. The man he had known then as Daniel Fallon.

"No?"

There was no response. Raider took Florette by the arm and turned him over. Florette did not resist. The tempered steel circles snapped closed over his wrists. Raider hauled him to his feet.

Carling took one of Florette's arms and Moore the other. They had to half support him as they eased him down the steps.

When the three of them were face to face with Manton, Manton raised his left hand to stop them. "A moment, please?"

"Sure."

Moore and Carling looked awkwardly away from the sight of this confrontation.

Raider did not.

He saw Manton reach up as if to touch Dane Florette on the cheek.

The pale, harried little man did not hurry. He reached up as if it were the most perfectly normal thing he had ever done.

Only at the last moment did Raider see a glint of light on steel as Manton's hand moved.

And the slender blade slide easily into the side of Dane Florette's neck. High on the left side. Into that vulnerable socket just beneath the ear.

With no emotion whatsoever, Eduard Manton nodded and stepped back away from his daughter's killer.

The bright blood spurted, spraying Charles Moore, who had hold of Florette's left arm. Carling grabbed for an unresisting Ted Manton. Raider's Remington came level again, this time aimed at Manton, but he could not bring himself to shoot.

Of them all, it was Dane Florette who seemed to take it the most calmly.

Florette looked at the man who had just killed him and laughed.

Then, his life's blood pouring onto the floor at his feet but awareness still in his eyes, he slumped forward. Carling and Moore eased him down and reached for Ted Manton.

"Wait," Raider said. "Leave it be."

"What?"

"Dane Florette died resisting arrest. If we all write it up that way in our reports, then Dane Florette died while resisting arrest, damn it."

"I'll damn sure swear to it," Carling said quickly.

Moore looked less willing.

Then he turned and looked up toward the top of the loft where Bernie Clawson and Bessie were huddled, crying together. Raider doubted that either of them was yet aware of what had happened those few feet away.

Moore grimaced. Then nodded. "The suspect had a knife. We struggled. He was accidentally stabbed with his own weapon. I can go along with that."

"Ted?" Raider asked.

Manton nodded. He was still staring blankly down at the dying Florette, the last flow of blood ebbing from him now onto the dusty stairs of the choir loft.

Raider went up to touch Clawson lightly on the shoulder, careful not to touch Bessie when he did so. "It's over," he said. "You can go home now. We can all go home."

Clawson nodded, barely aware of the others in his concern for Bessie, and let Raider guide him down the stairs and out into the cool freshness of the evening air.

Raider sat on the church steps after the father and daughter walked away in the twilight. He was in no hurry now. He felt . . . he thought about it for a moment. He felt sorrow. Not for Dane Florette. Not even for D. C. Florette Sr. The sorrow and regrets he felt were for Ted Manton.

Revenge, he knew, was not enough. But then for Dane Florette, no punishment ever could have been enough. Manton was going to learn that now. And the knowledge of it would haunt him forever.

Raider sighed and waited for the others to come outside.